★ Destiny ★

A week had passed since the night Claire so inventively handcuffed herself to the bed. And in that time his passion for her hadn't diminished, not in the least. In fact, it was the opposite. And ever since that night, he noticed things in ways he'd never noticed them before. Colors were more intense. Smells were more exotic.

At the moment he noticed the way the cold air felt on his face that was hot from cutting wood. The way the ground felt under his feet. The way his body felt, kind of light, kind of electric.

The way Claire felt.

Soft. Sweet.

Unbelievable.

Things happened for a reason. He firmly believed that. Why else would his plane have crashed in the middle of the mountains? Why else would he have ended up getting into *Claire's* Jeep?

It seemed to be his destiny.

BOOKS BY THERESA WEIR

American Dreamer
Cool Shade
Some Kind of Magic

Published by HarperPaperbacks

ATTENTION: ORGANIZATIONS AND CORPORATIONS

Most HarperPaperbacks are available at special quantity discounts for bulk purchases for sales promotions, premiums, or fund-raising. For information, please call or write:
Special Markets Department, HarperCollins Publishers, 10 East 53rd Street, New York, N.Y. 10022.
Telephone: (212) 207-7528. Fax: (212) 207-7222.

Some Kind of Magic

THERESA WEIR

HarperPaperbacks
A Division of HarperCollins*Publishers*

HarperPaperbacks
A Division of HarperCollinsPublishers
10 East 53rd Street, New York, N.Y. 10022-5299

If you purchased this book without a cover, you should be aware that this book is stolen property. It was reported as "unsold and destroyed" to the publisher and neither the author nor the publisher has received any payment for this "stripped book."

This is a work of fiction. The characters, incidents, and dialogues are products of the author's imagination and are not to be construed as real. Any resemblance to actual events or persons, living or dead, is entirely coincidental.

Copyright © 1998 by Theresa Weir
All rights reserved. No part of this book may be used or reproduced in any manner whatsoever without written permission of the publisher, except in the case of brief quotations embodied in critical articles and reviews. For information address HarperCollins*Publishers*, 10 East 53rd Street, New York, N.Y. 10022-5299.

ISBN 0-06-101295-5

HarperCollins®, 📖 ®, and HarperPaperbacks™ are trademarks of HarperCollins*Publishers*, Inc.

First printing: November 1998

Printed in the United States of America

Visit HarperPaperbacks on the World Wide Web at
http://www.harpercollins.com

❖ 10 9 8 7 6 5 4 3 2 1

To Pat and Helen—
for showing me the beauty that is Idaho

Some Kind of Magic

One

There were certain inevitabilities in life. Like the light at the end of the tunnel almost always being a train. Like the more you cared about people, the more likely you were to lose them.

Here was a new one.

The plane was going to crash.

Hmm, he thought. We're going to crash.

He'd never much cared for flying. Mostly because he liked being the one in control. He didn't like putting his life in someone else's hands. Now he guessed he could say that uneasy feeling he always got whenever he stepped into a plane wasn't entirely unfounded.

He wasn't scared. Maybe because his life had been nothing more than a series of screwups anyway.

A plane crash was probably as good a way to go as any. And sometimes enough was enough.

He had to give the pilot credit. He fought it

all the way down, somehow managing to keep the plane parallel to the ground until they were skimming along the snow-covered earth like a rock over water.

Trees were sheared.

Metal ripped.

The plane's right wing snapped away, then the left. With a huge roar, everything came to a bone-jarring halt.

Two

Claire Maxfield and her friend Libby sat in a dark corner of The Brewery, an ancient establishment with long wooden tables that had known the elbows of several generations of Fallon, Idaho, residents.

They were both on their second beer when the tone of the television in the corner changed. The regularly scheduled program was interrupted with another update on a twin-engine plane that had crashed that morning in the nearby mountains.

Libby leaned halfway across the table. "I heard one of the passengers is an escaped convict."

"Who told you that?" Claire asked, not believing her for an instant. Libby was always trying to manufacture calamity in her life. Nothing ever happened in Fallon, not in the winter anyway. In the summer, when tourists invaded the town and increased the population from two thousand to fifteen thousand, things happened, but those things were more along the line of bicycle thefts and public intoxication.

"Glenna, the girl who works mornings at the gas station—well, her brother-in-law is on the rescue team, and I overheard Glenna telling somebody that shots had been fired." Libby looked past Claire, momentarily distracted from the local gossip. "Here we go," she said with an air of expectancy.

A flaming cake suddenly appeared in front of Claire. One of those little emergency jobs.

Normally a cake would be the signal for waitresses to appear from every corner of the tavern, drawn like moths to a porch light. Instead, an approaching storm had sent most of the customers and staff scurrying home for the warmth of their own fires.

So the bartender came over, giving them a tenor for the requisite Happy Birthday sing-along.

When they were finished, the waitress apologized. "We couldn't fit thirty candles on the cake, so we just put on ten."

Libby got quite a kick out of that. Claire rolled her eyes.

"Make a wish!"

"Yeah, make a wish," everyone chimed.

Claire made a wish.

She blew.

There was a collective moan as all but one of the candles went out.

Claire blew again, extinguishing the lonely flame.

"Aw," the waitress moaned. "Now your wish won't come true."

"Gee, and I wished I could be fat, poor, and ugly." Claire wondered if she was getting drunk on two beers. It could happen.

"Really, what'd you wish for?" Libby asked a few minutes later around a mouthful of cake.

"For some excitement in my life." Not gossip-generated excitement, but *real* excitement.

"Don't we all." It was a statement, not a question.

They'd been friends a long time. Through diets and binges. Divorce and desertion.

They were friends, yes, but Claire was enough of a realist to know that it wasn't the kind of relationship where Libby would be there no matter what. If something—or some*one*—more exciting came along, Libby would vanish, to resurface months later, walking back into Claire's life as if she'd only just left.

Yet their friendship had endured. And maybe that's what it was all about. Endurance.

Claire understood that Libby had to have colors and noise, while Claire just liked to visit that place from time to time.

There was only once when their friendship had been seriously tested. That's when Libby had confessed that she'd seen all the Ernest movies—and liked them.

"You need to get out there," Libby said. "Start dating."

Claire took another swallow of beer. It was tasting better all the time.

Dating.

The word gave Claire chills.

"When I wished for excitement, I didn't mean a man. Excitement can be a good book. Or a new bar of scented soap. A good night of TV viewing. So good that I have to record one show while I'm watching another."

"You have high expectations, don't you?"

"If you don't ask, you won't receive."

"Anton's been gone, what, three months?"

It seemed like three years. And it seemed like three days. To Claire's humiliation, she was living a cliché. The one about the man who went out for cigarettes and never came back. Except in her case he'd gone to an artist retreat in California, met an independently wealthy widow, and never came home. He'd even managed to get one of his horrid oil paintings on the cover of a new magazine, *California Nights*.

After the years Claire had toiled to be able to accurately reproduce images on paper, all Anton had done was slap some bright colors on canvas and sleep with a rich woman.

It was hard on the self-esteem, getting dumped like that.

"Before I forget, I want you to start saving your glass bottles for me," Libby said, tearing Claire away from her morose musings.

"Recycling?" she asked.

Libby's eyes took on an excited glow that didn't appear to have anything to do with the beer she'd consumed. She leaned closer. "This spring I'm putting up a cement wall around my house. I have to have enough bottles to stick in the top. Then, after the cement hardens, you break the bottles so it leaves a jagged edge."

"How lovely," Claire murmured, not surprised in the least.

Libby's new thing was what Claire called compounding. For six months, she'd been working to make her home self-contained and as inaccessible as possible. Claire wasn't sure who her friend thought was coming, but whenever Libby got involved in a project, she went all the way and then some.

"When society collapses, you can come live with me. I've made sure I have enough stockpiled for my friends."

"Thanks. Just don't start wearing camo."

Libby got a strange look on her face—a confession, if ever Claire saw one.

"Oh, Libby."

"It's just one pair of field trousers. They're so comfortable. You should try them."

"I'll pass." More camouflage. Just what Idaho needed. "Don't you think the broken glass might be a little much?"

"I wouldn't talk if I were you."

"Me? I'm not the one building a wall."

"Oh, yeah?" Libby took another drink of beer. "Claire, he's not coming back."

"I know that. Even if he did, I wouldn't let him in the house."

"Yeah. Right."

"You think you know me so well."

Was she that weak? *Would* she take him back? It was true that she spent a large portion of her day fantasizing about Anton's return. Sometimes she slammed the door in his face. But most of the time she jumped into his arms, and pretty soon he was doing all the wild, wonderful things to her that he was so good at. She had to give him credit. He was definitely an artist when it came to making love.

"Last call," the bartender announced from across the room. A polite way of saying, Please leave.

"Oh, I almost forgot." Libby pulled two white paper bags from her backpack and slid them across the table. "I know you said no presents, but when I saw these, I had to get them. Open the little one first."

Claire was down to her last pair of Levi's, and they were ripped in more than one place. Two days ago, Libby had tried to talk Claire into letting her buy her a new pair of jeans for a birthday gift, but Claire had refused. She had pride. She may have been broke, but nobody was going to buy her clothes, not even Libby.

Thankfully the packages she'd shoved toward her were both too small to contain jeans. She didn't want to have to argue with Libby, especially when she was only trying to be nice.

She opened the sack Libby had indicated—and pulled out a small, rather crude stuffed doll with printing on it. *What in the world?* She remembered that it was a gift and that Libby was waiting for her reaction. Claire tried to compose her features, tried to act as if she really liked it, as if it were something she'd wanted. Whatever the hell it was.

"It's a voodoo doll."

Claire continued to stare, kind of fascinated, kind of horrified.

Libby pointed to the doll's tummy. "It has all the places marked where you can stick the pins. "And see—" She turned it over. "The other side has good voodoo."

"Good voodoo? I didn't know there was such a thing."

"Oh, *yeah*."

An Acme voodoo doll.

Libby turned it back over.

"You get some of Anton's hair, like out of a brush or something, and you glue it to the doll's head, then you poke these black pins in the different places. Here's the spot to make him impotent."

Since it hadn't yet been activated with anybody's hair, Claire felt fairly safe in testing a few pins in various sites. It almost made her feel as good as the time she'd burned all of Anton's silk underwear.

"Open the other one," Libby reminded her.

Claire was afraid to see what could possibly be next. She doubted anything could top the voodoo doll.

She was wrong.

The other present turned out to be a set of handcuffs.

Libby burst out laughing while Claire stared at the cuffs that were connected with about four feet of chain.

"They're called belly cuffs," Libby told her when she was able to catch her breath. "I got them at the army surplus store. They were right next to the grenades."

Claire didn't know what to say, so she fell back on the standard reply. "Just what I've always wanted. How did you know?"

Libby waved her hand, not believing her for a second. "If I know you, you'll use them to chain yourself to your easel."

Clare stuck both gifts in her purse. "We'd better get out of here before they tell us to leave." She slid across the slick vinyl seat. It wasn't until she stood up that she realized she was a little woozy.

When Anton left her, she'd tried drowning her sorrows, but all she ended up with was an evening of paying homage to the toilet bowl and a day in bed with a hangover. That's all it had taken for her to decide to leave the drama of the bottle to somebody else—somebody who could hold her liquor.

Standing, they both went about the chore of

putting on layers of winter crap, with Claire finishing by cramming a stocking cap on her head.

She felt about as sexy as a polar bear.

"You still have that cap?" Libby asked as they walked toward the door, waving goodnight to the bartender. "I swear I'm going to burn it one of these days."

Claire just gave her a sleepy smile.

Outside, the frigid air felt good on her hot cheeks. It stole her breath. It stung her eyes. More importantly, it cleared her head.

Without lingering, they said their good-byes through frozen lips, then scurried to their vehicles, the packed snow creaking under their boots, the way snow did when the temperature dropped to zero.

The Jeep's engine was sluggish, but it finally turned over.

Shivering, her breath a cloud in front of her face, Claire waited for the vehicle to warm up. Libby didn't dally. Instead, she honked her horn and took off, in a hurry to get to the safety of her compound.

That was when Claire thought she heard a sound, coming from directly behind her.

Her scalp tingled.

"Anton?"

In one of her daydreams, before she found out that Anton had left her for the old broad, she'd imagined him returning to her, injured and helpless. She would nurse him back to health so they could once again make passionate love.

She was beginning to think that the sound behind her seat had been nothing more than the ringing of her own ears, when something cold and hard pressed against the back of her head.

Her heart stopped.

Claire had never had a gun pressed to her head, or any other part of her body, but if she had, she was fairly certain it would feel like this. Exactly like this.

Cold.

Hard.

Any remnant of alcohol in her blood vanished. She went from warm fuzzy glow to completely sober in a fraction of a second.

A voice came out of the darkness directly behind her.

"Drive."

Not Anton.

Anton's voice was soft, sexy, sensual. This person's was harsh, broken.

Desperate.

She swallowed. Or tried to swallow. "Y-You c-can have my J-Jeep."

The gun was shoved more insistently against her head. "Shut up. Just shut up and do what I say."

Happy birthday, Claire.

She'd wished for excitement, but being taken hostage wasn't what she'd had in mind.

Was this what happened if you didn't blow out all your candles?

Three

"Haul ass."

At the moment, that particular part of her anatomy, plus every other part, was immobilized by fear. Both hands, bound in thick mittens, gripped the steering wheel, Claire's tight, shallow breathing creating a fog in front of her face, a layer of frost on the inside of the windshield.

Get out of the Jeep.

Barely minutes ago, Claire had been bemoaning the utter vacuousness of her life. Now her brain was scrambling over plans, rejecting them one after the other as she tried to come up with something to save herself.

Run.

She had a mittened hand on the doorhandle ready to bail when the man's arm shot out and wrapped around her throat, pulling her back against the seat, the barrel of the gun shoved under her earlobe.

"Don't go anywhere."

The words were forced out, one at a time against the vulnerable skin of her cheek, his breath whispered across her face, his unshaven jaw rough against her delicate skin. "I need you."

Even in her terror, it was impossible to miss the exhaustion and pain in his voice.

There had been a couple of times in Claire's life when she'd been so cold that every inch of her body trembled. He was shaking like that now.

The arm around her throat was shaking. The barrel pressed to her head—shaking.

That could be good.

Or that could be bad.

Maybe he was nervous about what he was doing. Maybe that meant he had a conscience. Or maybe it meant he was fighting the urge to kill her.

Either way, an involuntary twitch of his trigger finger could put an abrupt end to the drudgery of her days. And at the moment, the drudgery of her days was looking pretty appealing.

He smelled like gasoline and smoke. Not wood smoke, but something more toxic, something more like the smoke created by burning tires.

Her life didn't flash before her eyes, at least not in a linear way. But in a matter of a few elastic seconds she thought about the people she'd known, she thought about the things she wished she'd said, and the things she wished she hadn't.

Regrets.

She wished she'd had more guts in her life. She wished she'd taken more risks.

She wished she'd known love. Real love. Not the selfish, one-sided relationship she'd had with Anton.

"Drive!"

He shoved away from her, falling against the backseat.

Her lungs released the air she'd been holding. Her breath came out in one long, gasping sob.

Drive.

He'd told her to drive, and she would drive.

If only she could.

Her circulatory system had gone haywire, seizing up like the rest of her. Her fingers were so stiff she couldn't feel them anymore. Her teeth were knocking together hard enough to shatter.

It took her forever to get the Jeep into gear. As soon as the wheels began to turn, as soon as the vehicle began to move forward, she realized she couldn't see. She turned on the defroster, tepid air blasting her in the face. With her mittens, she scraped at the glass.

It didn't help.

Using her teeth, she tugged a mitten from one hand, then scraped at the ice with her fingernails, clearing a jagged circle big enough to see through.

Where was she supposed to go?

She asked the question, disgusted with herself for the obvious terror she failed to keep from her voice.

"Away . . . from . . . this fucking Siberia."

His words were broken, forced out through frozen lips. "Turn up the heat and head to your house."

Her house? Had he said *her* house? Why? She would have thought he'd want a ride to some buddy's place, or maybe some private airstrip. Her house hadn't even entered the realm of possibilities.

Okay. She got it now. This was something devised by Libby. Once they reached Claire's, the guy in the backseat would whip out his boom box and start stripping.

She relaxed a little. She may have even smiled slightly. "We don't need to go all the way to my place," she said over her shoulder. "Nothing personal, but I don't really want to see you take off your clothes. So let's just forget it. When Libby asks me about it, I'll tell her you were great."

"What the hell are you babbling about?"

"Libby hired you, right?"

"You're hurting my head. Just shut up and drive."

She tensed again. Libby hadn't hired him. This was real.

She couldn't take him to her house. Her house was too secluded, too remote. And she didn't have a phone. It wasn't that she was into the suffering artist thing. Even if she could afford a phone, she wouldn't have one. Born too soon or too late, she wanted to see a person's face when she spoke with him or her. Half of a conversation was facial expressions. It was too hard, too unnatural with just the voice.

She could go to Libby's—but no, the last thing she wanted to do was expose her friend to danger. *Forgive me, Libby. That wall with the jagged glass doesn't seem nearly so wacko now.*

The police station? What about the police station?

It wouldn't take a genius to catch on if she pulled up in front of a building that had a couple of patrol cars out front and bars on the windows. She didn't want to do anything to set him off.

Maybe her house wasn't such a bad idea. She would have the advantage since she knew the layout. It could be like Audrey Hepburn in *Wait Until Dark.*

She felt faint. Dizzy.

Hot air blasted her in the face. She turned down the temperature gauge.

"Turn that up. I'm freezing my ass off back here."

She turned it back up, sweat trickling down her spine, under her layers upon layers of winter clothing.

"I'm not going to hurt you," he said thickly. "I just want a place to get warm. Get some dry clothes. A place to . . ." His words trailed off, as if he were having trouble concentrating. "Think. A place . . . to . . . think."

She felt a pang of sympathy, a feeling she pushed to the back of her mind.

His exhaustion was obvious. If she took him to her house, maybe he would fall asleep. If that happened, she could get away. She could go for help.

"My husband's home," she said, trying one last time to change his mind.

"Shut up and drive."

The tone of his voice told her that he was tired of her chatter.

And so she drove.

In the direction of her house.

She'd read somewhere that kidnappers thought of their victims as nonpeople. And as soon as they began to think of them as people, things changed. There was much less chance of their harming you.

"What's your name?" she asked over her shoulder, cringing, hoping he didn't consider her question too personal.

He didn't respond right away.

"Dylan," he finally said.

It had taken him too long to come up with an answer.

"Mine's Claire."

"Claire." There was hesitation as he seemed to give that some thought. "Is that a hillbilly name?"

In his book, was hillbilly good or bad? "I don't know," she said, playing it safe.

"I've heard about you mountain people. You marry your cousins and brothers and shit like that."

"I think you've watched a few too many daytime talk shows," she said, anger beginning to edge away her terror.

"You know what I think?" he asked. "I think you made up that stuff about a husband." He sniffed the air. "You have that mothball smell about you that says you live alone."

A mothball smell! How could she smell like mothballs?

But then she remembered that before meeting Libby at the tavern, she'd been to the nursing home to talk to the administrator about the art classes she was going to teach. Had some of that old smell rubbed off on her?

"Do you gargle with Listerine and drink castor oil?" he asked.

How old did he think she was?

"What's your last name? Clampett?" He kind of laughed a little to himself, as if getting a kick out of his own joke.

"Maxfield," she said. People often accused her of making it up, deliberately naming herself after Maxfield Parrish, the American painter, or Peter Max, but Maxfield was the name on her birth certificate.

"What did you do?" she asked, still attempting to get him to open up.

"Do?" he asked reflectively. "I was born."

"I mean, what are you running from?"

"Maybe I'm just running from myself."

She ignored his evasive answer. "There's nowhere you can go. Nowhere you can hide. Why don't I drive you to the police station? They'll be easier on you if you turn yourself in."

"You're the one who's been watching too much TV."

Twenty miles.

That's how far it was from Fallon to Claire's house. Maybe it would give her time to come up with a plan.

Behind her he'd fallen silent. Five minutes later there was still no sound from the backseat.

Was he asleep?

She gradually slowed the Jeep. When the speedometer dropped to thirty, she reached for the doorhandle. She would jump. She would jump and she would land in a snowdrift, and she would be okay.

Behind her, he stirred.

She let go of the doorhandle and pressed a booted foot back down on the accelerator.

Ten minutes later, she pulled up in front of the two-story log home she rented during the off-season. The automatic yard light came on, illuminating a path to the door.

Under normal conditions, she would have been glad to be home. Now she was afraid she'd driven herself into a trap.

Claire cut the engine and pocketed the keys, grabbed her purse and slipped from the Jeep.

The man was right behind her.

He tumbled out the door, sprawling at her feet.

She let out a surprised, sympathetic sound. Her reaction was automatic. A human in trouble. She reached for him.

He growled low in his throat and jerked away. "Leave me alone." Without assistance, he lurched to his feet, then stood there swaying, getting his bearings as he looked in the direction of the house.

Suddenly Claire's dog, Hallie, decided it was time to punch in. She erupted from her fiberglass igloo, barking frantically.

Dylan—if that really was his name, and Claire sincerely doubted it—let out an alarmed shout. With gun in hand, he swung to face the dog.

The gun wobbled.

Claire threw herself on Hallie, hugging the shepherd to her. "Don't hurt her!" Hallie may have come out barking, but it was all a front. She was one of the biggest cowards of the dog world.

"For chrissake, lady." There was blatant irritation in the man's voice. "I'm not going to hurt your dog."

Relieved, Claire let go of the dog and got to her feet.

"You leave your dog outside in this Siberia?"

"She's used to it," Claire said defensively. "She'd get too hot inside. I let her inside sometimes. If it's really cold." She couldn't believe he was chastising her over the care of her dog.

"Quit blathering and open the door."

He was hugging himself, shaking.

Claire unlocked the door, her mind racing. She stepped back, hoping he would go first and she could make a run for it. Instead, she felt his hand on her back, pushing her in ahead of him.

She felt for the wall switch, muted light from a forty-watt bulb cast shadows about the room.

She dropped her purse on the kitchen table and turned to get her first good look at her captor.

Everything hit her at once. The cut and bruise on his forehead; the dark, intense gaze; the broad, unshaven jaw; the sensual mouth, with softly curving lips.

"My God," she said.

Claire had an eye for detail. After all, she was an artist. Maybe. Unfortunately the verdict was still out on that. But if she were to witness a robbery, she'd be able to tell the police what the thief looked like from the top of his head to the color of his shoelaces. She didn't try to figure out why a person would, say, wear a golf cap with a suit, she simply observed the phenomenon.

It wasn't light enough in the room to distinguish the color of the man's eyes, but they were looking at her with an unwavering directness that she found disconcerting. The cut across his forehead had bled, then dried. He may have tried to clean his face at some time or another, but hadn't had much success. His jacket was torn, white feathers oozing out the rips. Some of the squares were flat and empty. His jeans were stained with what looked like blood—from his head?—and some kind of black soot, as if he'd stood too near a fire.

He was younger than she'd thought. Not over thirty, she'd guess.

He swayed, spotting the couch. He stumbled forward, falling into it, onto it, letting out a gasp of pain as he went down.

He just sat there awhile, apparently waiting for everything to stabilize, waiting for the sharp edges of his pain to dull.

Light from the kitchen fell on his face, accentuating the contrast of elegant bone structure. His hair was short and dark and straight. It was the kind of hair that had a mind of its own, that had a tendency to stick up around a cowlick. He had two: One on top of his head, to the side, and one in front, above his right eye. Near that right eye was a small, half-moon scar.

"The Jeep keys," he mumbled, holding out his hand. "Give 'em to me."

Claire fished them out of her pocket and dropped them into his outstretched palm.

Long fingers curled around them. "The other set. I want the other set, too."

"I don't have another set." She'd always been a terrible liar. Whenever she told a lie, she had an annoying tendency to smile; she didn't know why.

Anton. There was a guy who could lie. Almost as well as he made love. Maybe better.

"Don't bullshit me. Everybody has two sets of keys."

"I lost them." She felt a little tug at one corner of her mouth. "I swear."

"Get me a phone. I need a phone."

"I don't have one."

With that, his eyes pinned her right where she stood.

She swallowed.

"You're not old," was what he finally said, seeming to have momentarily forgotten about the phone. "I thought you were old."

Now he was looking at her in a strange way, in a speculative way.

She took a step back, her hand reaching blindly behind her. "Don't touch me," she said, her voice quivering.

He frowned, his thick, dark brows drawing together in a menacing way.

She put up a hand as if to hold him back, or deflect the bullet if he decided to use the gun. "Please think about what you're doing. You don't want to add rape to your crimes, do you?"

"What?"

His menacing expression changed. Now he

was staring at her as if the idea of sex with her was totally ludicrous.

She looked down at herself.

She was wearing a bulky barn jacket. Sticking out from under the jacket was the tattered hem of a wool sweater that just may have been giving off the mothball scent he'd mentioned earlier. Under that was her heavy Polartec. Under that was not one but two layers of long underwear. Then there was the pair of jeans Libby had begged Claire to let her replace, the ones with the slightly ripped crotch and the more severely ripped knee. The dismal jeans were tucked into a pair of heavy Sorrel boots.

Victoria's Secret, eat your heart out.

Topping off her ensemble was the stocking cap that one of the residents of Pineview Nursing Home had made for her. It was crocheted granny squares in about every lovely color not found in nature.

She reached up and pulled it off.

Her hair snapped with electricity. She felt it elevating about her head. She put the cap to her nose, but couldn't smell anything mothbally.

No, sex was probably the farthest thing from the man's mind.

"Sorry, honey." There was humor in his dark eyes.

He was laughing at her!

"I don't have it in me right now. Just get me a phone."

"I don't have one," she repeated.

His gaze moved around the cabin, momentarily stopping on the woodstove, the woodpile, the kerosene lamp that had come in handy on more than one occasion when the power had gone out, then finally coming back to her. "I can't believe I've gotten mixed up with some hippie, some back-to-nature freak with no phone."

She didn't care what he thought about her. She just wanted him and his gun out of there.

He smiled. "Somebody could come along and kidnap you, and you wouldn't be able to call anybody for help."

Her muscles began to unknot—now that she knew rape wasn't on the agenda, but she refused to laugh at his pathetic joke.

"If you don't have a phone, then get me some dry clothes. The sooner you do, the sooner I'll be out of here."

Thank God! Oh, thank God! She hurried from the room and quickly dug through some of Anton's abandoned clothes, ones she hadn't yet burned. Her visitor was taller, heavier compared to Anton's lithe frame. She ended up settling on a pair of jogging pants, plus a flannel shirt she'd given Anton last winter.

He'd hated it.

She also came up with a pair of striped boxer shorts, a white T-shirt, and a pair of heavy wool socks.

When she stepped back into the living room,

the man had stripped to the waist. The right side of his torso, above the rib cage, was one huge, massive bruise.

"You need a doctor." It was merely an observation. She didn't care if he got medical attention. After all, he's kidnapped her at gun point.

"Just gimme the clothes."

She threw the bundle on the couch.

He unbuttoned his jeans, then reached for the zipper.

On his arm was a strange tattoo, below the tattoo, writing that she couldn't make out. A gang symbol?

"If you don't want to get an eyeful, I suggest you turn around." Without waiting for her to comply, he began peeling off his pants.

She remained where she was, not wanting to turn her back on him.

"But then, maybe you do want to get an eyeful. That's okay with me. I'm not modest."

She slowly turned away. She took three steps when he stopped her.

"Stay here. Where I can see you."

She waited, her ears fine-tuned. She heard the sound of boots hitting the floor, heard the sound of fabric moving over skin.

She imagined him slipping into the shorts, the pants, the shirt.

Until she became aware of the silence behind her.

She waited.

And waited.

Then slowly turned in time to see him collapse on the couch.

Sitting, he lunged for the nearest receptacle, which happened to be the kindling bucket, his gun clattering to the floor. With one hand to his stomach, the other gripping the bucket, he threw up.

When he was finished, he retrieved the gun and fell back against the couch, eyes tightly closed, breathing shallow, his skin the color of paste. The plaid shirt was yet to be buttoned, the tails lying across his thighs.

"Do something with that," he whispered.

If he hadn't given her such a direct order, Claire would have had no problem complying. As it was, Claire had a problem with people trying to tell her what to do. "No."

"I've got a gun."

"I won't clean up after you."

"Shit." He got to his feet, grabbed the bucket, shuffled to the front door, put the bucket outside, and let the dog in.

He made it back to the couch, Hallie following, tail wagging, her body language seeming to ask, Am I supposed to be doing this? Even if I'm not, I like it.

With his eyes closed, the man jammed the gun into the waistband of the gray jogging pants.

Claire stared. And stared some more.

At his pallor. At his face that needed to be

shaved. At the gun jammed into his pants. Why did men put guns there? It didn't seem like a good idea.

For a guy, it was like putting a gun to his head.

A hysterical giggle rose in her throat. She put a hand to her mouth, trying to stop it.

Too late.

Dark, hooded eyes flew open. They were gray. She could see that now. "What's so damn funny?"

"Isn't that kind of cold?" She pointed to the weapon in question.

It took him a moment to figure out what she was talking about. When he did, irritation flashed across his features—his reaction to such an inane question. He had bigger problems than cold metal against his belly.

"No," he said slowly. "Haven't you heard? Happiness is a warm gun."

Four

*

"What else do you need? Food? Money?" Claire wanted him out of there as quickly as possible.

"I changed my mind. I'm not leaving."

"What?"

"Not leaving."

"You said you'd leave if I got you some clothes."

"I lied."

She shouldn't have been surprised.

"Get me some rope."

"Rope?" She shook her head. "Oh, I'm sure I don't have anything like that around. I wouldn't have any use for rope. Never use rope."

He cast a quick glance around the room, his gaze falling to the floor where an extension cord trailed to a nearby table lamp. He took three steps, bent, and unplugged the cord at both ends, then began moving in her direction.

She shook her head, her eyes locked with his. "Don't tie me up. Please don't tie me up."

"Come on. Hands behind your back."

"Hallie! Attack!" Claire pointed at the dog's supposed prey.

Sleepy from the unaccustomed heat, Hallie just thumped her tail against the floor.

"Get him! Get him, girl!"

Hallie got to her feet and stood there smiling, her tail wagging, but Claire could tell she wanted nothing more than to lie back down.

How could she not understand the urgency of the situation? Weren't dogs supposed to have a sixth sense?

Claire gave up and tried another tactic. "I— uh . . . I have to go to the bathroom."

He was looking at her in a disgusted manner. As if he'd heard that line a million times.

"I *do*."

She shifted from one foot to the other, to prove her point. The problem was, now that she thought about it, she *did* have to go. She recalled the beer she'd drunk at The Brewery. Looking back, it seemed like days ago, but her bladder had a different spin on it.

Bored and thankful to be out of the limelight, Hallie returned to her spot near the door, circled a few times, then lay back down.

"If you remember correctly," she said, "I was at a tavern. I had a couple of beers. You know how beer goes through you."

Finally something he seemed able to relate to. "Okay." He pulled the gun from the waistband of his pants and motioned her away. "But I'm coming along. And no shutting the door."

She stared at him, dumbfounded. No way was she going to the bathroom with him watching her.

"If you're afraid I'm going to get turned on by some mothball-smelling woman taking a pee, you're nuts. Go on." He motioned with the gun again.

She really had to go. Bad.

"Okay, but keep your back to me. Don't look."

"Believe me. You don't have anything I want to see."

And so he kept guard at the bathroom door, his body slightly turned to the side, his back not completely toward her. But it would have to do. At least he'd returned the gun to his waistband.

"You're not from around here," she said, trying to dredge up some form of conversation while she gingerly pulled down her pants, all the while keeping an eye on his back.

"How could you tell? Because I'm not attracted to my first cousin?"

She ignored that comment, concentrating on quickly getting the job done. "I'm not from around here either." Finished, she quickly pulled up her long underwear and jeans.

"And that makes us alike? Don't patronize me."

"I'm not— Don't turn around!"

Claire took a quick inventory of the sink. A can of deodorant and some hairspray she hadn't used in a month. She took a silent step to the left. Then another. She paused, then grabbed the deodorant, finger to the nozzle. Before she could chicken out, she jumped at him, holding down the button, the can aimed at his face, at his eyes. She let out a scream as she scored a direct hit. She continued to press the button, screaming in terror at his possible—probable—retaliation as the fog of spray hit him.

He let out a surprised yelp of his own. Or rather a cry of agony. Bent at the waist, he pressed the heels of both hands to his eyes.

She dropped the deodorant and bolted past him, knocking into him as she went. Two steps later, she was being tackled to the ground, the air rushing from her lungs as she made contact with the wooden floor, stomach first.

"Son of a bitch," he moaned, his body pinning hers to the floor.

He was mad. He was *furious*.

He writhed and bellowed on top of her.

She reached behind her and managed to grab a tuft of his cropped hair. She yanked.

He bellowed again, but didn't release his hold.

He jerked her fingers from his hair, quite a few strands coming with it, then proceeded to drag her across the floor to the dropped extension cord. The next thing she knew, his knee was in her spine, her arms were pinned behind her back, and he was wrapping the cord around her wrists. All the while, Hallie was watching, her mouth open in what looked like a happy smile.

"Normally," he said as he worked, his voice breathless, "I don't like to manhandle women. But I can say I'm actually enjoying this." He gave the cord another tug, then moved to the side. "Bend your knees and bring your feet up in the air."

She should have been afraid of him, terrified of him, but the only emotion she felt was anger at being treated so callously. Instead of bringing up her feet, she rolled to the side and kicked at him with her heavy boots, making satisfactory contact with his knee. He let out a grunt of surprise, shoved her hard to her stomach again, pulled her feet up and wound the rest of the cord around her until she lay there like a roped rodeo calf. Then he got to his feet and headed straight for the bathroom.

She heard water splashing in the sink. He must have been washing out his eyes.

"I hope they catch you and put you in a maximum security prison for the rest of your life!" she shouted. "I never used to believe in the death sentence!" She continued to shout so that he could hear her. "But your gentle manner has pretty much persuaded me to cast my vote in a new direction!"

She watched as he stepped out of the bathroom. Without a glance in her direction, he cut through the living room to disappear into the bedroom.

Ears straining for the slightest sound, she heard the creaking of the bed, heard him shifting his weight, getting more comfortable. Then silence.

What?

She listened and listened.

The silence gave way to gentle, rhythmic snoring.

She made a sound of frustration while trying to kick her feet, only managing to pull her bindings tighter.

"Hey, man. You alive?"

Was he dreaming? It seemed so real, like something that was actually happening.

"Hey, man. You alive?" the voice repeated.

No.

"Hey, man."

Dylan blinked, trying to focus. He couldn't. There was something in his eyes.

Blood. He had blood in his eyes.

"I'm gonna go for help. Okay? You hear me?"

Darkness sucked him down, sucked him in, swallowed him.

Dark. So dark . . .

Later, he came to.

Cold.

He tried to get to his feet.

He couldn't.

Something held him down.

A seat belt.

With frozen fingers, he struggled with the catch, finally feeling the belt slip away. On weak legs, he stood. With a heavy thud, something fell to the floor near his feet.

A gun.

He put out a hand to steady himself, grabbing the back of the pilot's seat, his fingers coming in contact with fabric.

Jesus. The pilot. He was still in the plane. Slumped over the controls.

Dead?

Keeping his head bent beneath the low ceiling, he picked up the man's wrist to feel for a pulse.

He let go.

The body was already stiff.

How much time had passed?

He turned away, feeling sick to his stomach. He bent and picked up the gun, then shuffled to the doorway. He jumped, his legs giving out when he hit the ground, the snow swallowing him.

Claire rolled around on the cold, hard floor, too pissed off to care that she was bruising herself.

All she'd accomplished in the last several hours was to cut off the circulation in her arms.

Okay.

Calm down.

You can do this.

She rested. The relaxation of her muscles created slack in the bonds.

It was only an extension cord—an old, thin one at that. How tough was an old, thin extension cord?

She wormed her way across the floor until she was next to the woodstove. Maneuvering into position, she rubbed the stretched cord against the cast-iron edge of the stove. After a minute, the cord snapped. In familiar territory now—she and the neighbor kids used to play this game all the time—Claire brought her legs through the circle made by her arms, so that her hands were in front of her. Then, using her teeth, she went to work on the bindings around her wrists.

The bed was so soft. So damn soft . . . Like snow. Deep, deep snow . . .

Dylan was lying in the snow, contemplating life, when he thought he heard the sound of voices. He raised his arm, hoping to get their attention.

Something smacked into the tree, just inches above his head. Bark flew.

That's weird.

He heard another *pop*. More bark flew.

That's when he realized the assholes were shooting at him.

He staggered to his feet—and tumbled head-first over the edge of an embankment.

Five

Pain.

That was the first thing Dylan was aware of.

The second was the groggy realization that the mothball woman was standing in the doorway, a gun—*his* gun—in her hand, pointing it at his head.

He squinted, trying to bring her into focus. All he could make out was shiny dark hair.

Last night, when he'd watched her come out of the tavern all bundled up, wearing that silly-ass hat, he'd figured she had to be at least a hundred.

But then later, he'd noticed her hair. Noticed the way it reflected light. Like a kid's.

It had looked so soft, still holding the magic of innocence and youth. He'd wanted to touch it.

For a moment, her hair had taken him back, reminding him of his fleeting childhood.

Sorrow could be sharp. Sorrow could be

dull. But the sudden stab of bittersweet longing took him by surprise, made him pull in a quick, aching breath.

Last night, he'd had every intention of waking up to untie her. He'd never meant to leave her bound for very long. Just to teach her a lesson.

But it seemed he'd overslept.

So many mistakes. So many bad moves.

Life was hard.

And it kept getting harder.

Give him a playing field where everything was clear, where everyone did just what they were supposed to do. That's what he liked. He could handle that. But real life. It was like chess without the rules.

He shifted his hips against the mattress. He shoved himself to a sitting position. Son of a bitch. His side hurt like hell. He probably had a couple of cracked ribs. His head hurt even more.

Son of a bitch.

"Gotta go."

His voice sounded kind of sloppy, kind of thick, even to him.

He knew he had to keep moving, knew someone was after him, but he couldn't remember why.

"Who are you?" she asked, the gun still pointing at his head.

"Who am I?" he asked in a contemplative voice. Good question. "You know who I am? I'm the guy who goes around to all the hand dryers in all the gas stations of the world, and once I find those dryers, I take out my trusty pocket knife and scratch the immortal words, Wipe Hands on Panties." He paused, waiting.

She didn't say anything, but she looked confused as hell.

"Impressed?" he asked. "You should be."

That confused her even more. Join the club. It confused him, too. But it was funny. Just funny as hell. He laughed, then quickly stopped.

God, his head hurt.

He wished the room would quit swirling.

"Gotta hit the road."

"I'm holding a gun on you."

"That's okay. I still gotta go. Got places to go, people to meet." What the hell was he talking about? "But you gotta watch out." He waggled a finger at her. "I want you to know it was only because of my tactical skills that I was able to outmaneuver and beat them at their own game."

"Beat who?"

His head was spinning. He felt drunk. He thought about his work. Thought about the people he'd taken out. He hated it, hated his life and what he had become. "I'm an assassin, you know," he said confidentially. It was true. That's what his life had been reduced to. "I'm nothing more than a hired gun."

He heard her quick intake of breath. She was scared of him. He was sorry about that. But a lot of people were scared of him. He shoved himself to his feet and stood there swaying, the pain in his side mind-numbing, his head screaming.

He began to move toward her.

"Stay back."

She jabbed at the air with the gun, holding it with both hands, taking a step away from him.

He caught up with her, backing her into a dresser beside the door. The scent of her hair stopped him for a brief second. Without conscious thought, he lifted a piece of that shimmering sweetness to his cheek, the strands snagging on his unshaven jaw. He closed his eyes and inhaled.

And inhaled again.

God, but she smelled good.

Dylan opened his eyes to see the barrel of the gun just inches from his nose. He pulled back a little, so things weren't so blurry. Past the barrel of the gun was a pair of blue-green eyes, looking scared, looking nervous.

Now she looked more like a little kid than any old lady.

"Who takes care of you?" he asked, curious, concerned.

"What?" The word held astonishment, as if she couldn't quite believe what she'd heard.

"Who takes care of you?" he repeated.

The gun barrel quit its wavering. "I take care of myself."

"A queen is strong, but she still needs a knight."

The room tilted. His legs felt rubbery. He let go of her hair and dropped his arm.

He was thirsty.

Damn thirsty.

He pushed past her and headed in the direction of the kitchen.

In the refrigerator, he found what he was looking for: water. He unscrewed the cap and lifted the bottle to his mouth.

He was still guzzling the water when he heard a *click*. It was the sound of a pistol being cocked.

"Get out of my house," the mothball woman demanded. *"Now."*

He continued to drink, water running down his chin until he polished off the entire bottle. He wiped his mouth with the back of his hand.

Had he taken the bullets out of the gun? He couldn't remember. Wished to hell he could remember.

He was losing it.

He watched her as she stood there, the gun shaking all over the place.

And as he stood there staring at her, he got the oddest urge.

To kiss her.

Which was weird as hell, considering the fact that she was pointing a gun at his head.

He smiled at her.

He could see that that worried her even more. "W-Why are you looking at me like that?" she asked. "Quit looking at me like that."

Instead of kissing her, he walked past her and found his coat on the couch where he'd left it. He shrugged into it, grimacing at his bruised ribs. He'd forgotten about them. It was hard to keep track of everything. There was just so damn much going on.

"What are you doing?"

She'd followed him.

"Leaving."

He didn't feel quite as dizzy.

He crossed the room. When he opened the door, cold air hit him full in the face, reviving him.

Hell, he was okay.

The storm that weathermen had been predicting for days finally hit.

Heedless of the thickly falling snow, Claire watched in disgust as Hallie followed the man to her battered Jeep. "Here Hallie." Holding the gun in one hand, she slapped the other hand against her thigh. "Come here, Hallie."

Hallie ignored her and continued to smile her adoring dog smile directly at the very primate who'd abducted her mistress.

Claire watched as he stuck the key in the ignition. Watched as he started the engine. Watched as he tried to pull away. The Jeep died and he had to start it again. Then again.

"I'll shoot you!" she shouted, grasping the

butt of the revolver with both hands, assuming a serious stance with legs braced apart.

He reversed, stuck the Jeep into first, and spun away, the tires sliding in the rapidly building snow.

Claire watched as her Jeep, her one connection to the outside world, disappeared around the corner.

"*Damn.*"

She lowered the gun.

Well, at least he was gone. That was the important thing.

She thought about the way he'd smiled at her, a secret kind of smile, a smile that had scared her, that had made her heart flutter. And then she looked at Hallie, who was staring down the deserted road as if her doggy heart had been broken. Claire walked up to her and patted her head. "I guess we've both got rotten taste in men."

An hour later, Claire was wolfing down a breakfast bar when her gaze landed on the purse she'd dropped on the kitchen table last night. She opened it and pulled out the voodoo doll.

Hmm.

A woman on a mission of revenge, she jumped to her feet and hurried to the bedroom, to the bed to examine the pillow where the felon had rested his head. She found a couple of straight dark hairs about two inches long.

Excited, she returned to the kitchen and quickly found a squeeze container of school glue. With the glue, she attached the hair to the doll's head. Then she turned the voodoo doll over to the bad side, found a black needle, and jabbed it into the doll's head, at the temple.

With one hand on the wheel, Dylan tugged off his jacket, trying to ignore the pain in his side.

He felt dizzy again. He rolled down the window and stuck his head partway out, doing the dog thing. It didn't help. He pulled his head back in.

He blinked, trying to see through the falling snow.

He blinked again. It was a slow blink this time. An I-can-hardly-keep-my-eyes-open kind of blink.

When he opened his eyes again, there was a tree, a huge evergreen tree in the middle of the road.

It didn't move when he hit it.

Six

☾

The first thing Claire did was lock the door. Then she had to immediately unlock it to feed Hallie. After putting out fresh food and water, she relocked the door, then went around the entire cabin making sure the back door and windows, even the upstairs windows in the loft were locked.

Then she spent some meaningful time staring at the gun she'd left lying on the kitchen table next to her purse and box of generic bran flakes. She was no weapons expert—only having been given a crash course from Libby, who'd been trying to get Claire to buy a handgun for years, but she finally figured out how to remove the cartridge.

It was empty.

With the cartridge out of the way, she squinted down the chamber, the barrel pointing away from her. It was empty, too.

She'd been abducted and held hostage with a gun that wasn't even loaded. There was no sense in giving Dylan the benefit of the doubt. It was highly likely that he hadn't known there were no more bullets in it.

She took the gun upstairs, to the loft. The loft wasn't the handiest place to get to. It had once had spring-loaded wooden steps attached to a door that you pulled down from the ceiling. When that contraption went on the blink, the owners replaced it with a ten-foot stepladder. Claire actually liked it. To her, it made the loft seem a little like a tree house.

She ended up wrapping the gun in an old, soft T-shirt and hiding it in the back of a bottom drawer that she used for art supplies. Then she went back downstairs and took a shower. While her hair dried, she turned on the TV. Five minutes into one of the morning programs, the local news broke in.

"A report just in on the private plane that crashed yesterday in the Sawtooth Mountains. The identity of the injured man, who walked ten miles to the nearest town to get help for his fellow passenger, is none other than reclusive chess champion Daniel French. As we reported earlier, the pilot was found dead. An interesting twist to the story is the identity of the other passenger, whom French says was alive when he left the plane to find help." The middle-aged announcer paused to listen to his earpiece. "Do we have that file photo? We do?" Back to the camera. "The other passenger is convicted felon Trevor Davis who made his escape from a maximum security prison two years ago while serving a fifteen-year sentence for embezzlement and fraud."

She *knew* his name wasn't Dylan.

A sketch appeared on the screen, a drawing of a man with dark aviator sunglasses and a hooded sweatshirt. It could have been anybody.

"If you see this man, do not approach him. He may be armed and dangerous. Instead, contact the Idaho state police."

Claire stared at the screen for quite a while before she realized the program had moved on to something new.

She had to get to a phone. She had to get to the police.

Claire was used to cold weather. And snow. And walking long distances. That was good, because the nearest neighbor was three miles across country, almost four if she stuck to the road. The Herman family. They were a spooky bunch, a father and his three sons, none of whom practiced good dental hygiene. Claire had run into them a few times, enough to know that they were suspicious and scared of the strange woman who lived alone.

That would be her.

Claire dressed in several layers of clothing, filled her backpack, then headed in the direction of the Herman homestead, sticking to the road because of the snow.

She had gone about a mile and a half when she spotted something near the side of the road. About fifty yards in front of her and to the right was a vehicle resting flush against the trunk of a pine tree. And that snow-covered vehicle looked suspiciously like her Jeep.

Claire waded through the deep snow, sinking to her thighs when she hit the ditch that ran along the road.

With mittened hands, she dug the snow away from the Jeep until she was able to open the door.

The cab was a dark cocoon.

An empty cocoon.

Except for Dylan's jacket. Correction— *Trevor's* jacket.

She circled the Jeep. The snow had already partially covered her tracks. Dylan's—Trevor's— were long gone.

She made another circle, this one bigger than the last.

She almost stepped on him.

Like her grandmother would have said, If he'd been a snake he would have bit her.

Trevor was lying on his back, his eyes closed, head bare.

She peeled off one of her mittens and felt his face.

Ice cold.

She placed two fingers against his neck, the way she'd been taught in CPR class.

He groaned. Slowly, he opened his eyes.

He didn't look good. Not good at all.

She found herself staring at his head, at the fresh cut on his forehead, an inch above the old one.

The voodoo doll.

No.

It couldn't have been. She didn't believe in such nonsense. If she did, she would never have done it. The pin-jabbing had merely been an outlet for her anger and frustration. She'd never meant to hurt him.

She visualized the doll, lying on the kitchen table where she'd left it, the black pin still in its little head.

She had to get back and remove the pin.

Trevor stared up at her with glassy eyes. His mouth moved as he struggled to form words, struggled to speak.

She leaned closer, straining to hear.

"Is this . . . hell?"

A simple question. A direct question.

"No," she told him. "It's Idaho."

He made a sound deep in his throat, something she thought may have been a laugh.

"I wanted to see snow," he said, snowflakes melting into the darkness of his eyes. She placed a mittened hand against his forehead, to shield his face.

"Nobody ever told me it'd be a fucking Siberia."

He'd already mentioned his touchingly quaint affinity for the area.

"Hey, I know you," he said, his eyes seeming to clear slightly. "You're Max."

"Max?"

"Maxfield, but I'll call you Max. I prefer one syllable names, don't you?"

"Like *Trev*?"

That didn't seem to sink in. His eyes were getting that vacant look again.

"We need to get you someplace warm," she said. "The Jeep is only a few feet away."

"It's shot."

"We might be able to get the heater going even if it can't be driven."

He rolled his head in denial. "Radiator's busted."

"Then you'll have to walk."

Unfortunately her house was the nearest shelter by over a mile.

"Can't walk."

"You *have* to."

He reached up, placing frozen fingers against her cheek. "I feel like shit," he explained.

"It's not that far."

"My head hurts. I have a headache." To further emphasize its severity, he added, "A shit big headache."

He took his hand from her cheek, kind of waved it in the air until he found his own forehead. "Here. I hurt here."

Oh God. Had she done this to him?

He frowned, then looked around, as if unable

to figure out how he'd gotten there, as if he'd already forgotten who she was.

She tried not to let him see her fear. She didn't want to scare him. He would need every ounce of strength to get to shelter. "Your head will feel better as soon as you get inside. As soon as we get you someplace warm. My house isn't far," she lied. If he knew how far away it was, he would never even try. Let him think it was just around the next tree. "It's just a short walk." She grabbed his arm, trying to pull him to his feet.

Impossible.

"Get up, Trevor. *Please.*"

"You talkin' to me?"

"*Yes.*"

"Call me Dylan."

"Okay, Dylan. Get up. You have to get up."

"Okay, okay. Quit your naggin' an' I will. Just quit your naggin'."

It hurt to watch him.

Slowly, achingly, he rolled over to his stomach. Then, inch by inch, he managed to get his knees under him. With her arms around his waist, she helped to pull him upright.

Once there, he stood swaying, arms outstretched, trying to get his balance.

When he regained some equilibrium, they began moving forward through the snow, in the direction of the Jeep and his jacket, and then hopefully home and a warm fire.

Seven

Snow.
Everywhere.
Cold.

Dylan knew it was cold, but the temperature wasn't bothering him anymore. That was good.

The woman—Claire—was trying to make him stand, shoving him up against the Jeep, trying to hold him, her words breathless, like she'd been running or working hard.

He frowned, trying to focus, trying to concentrate on what she was saying.

He blinked, forcing his eyes to stay open. Everything was blurry. Little by little, Claire came into focus.

Her nose was red. Her cheeks were red. Her mouth was red.

Talking.

She was talking, her voice coming to him from somewhere beyond the wasteland of his semi-oblivion.

Stand up.

Okay. For her, okay.

He locked his knees, or at least he thought he did. He couldn't feel them. He couldn't feel anything. Ever since he'd stepped into the mothball woman's frozen world, he'd been numb.

Something was bothering him. Nagging at the back of his mind. He'd done something he felt guilty about.

Tied her up.

Pointed a gun at her.

"I—" He tried to talk, but his mouth, his lips felt weird as hell. Like he'd been Novocained.

"Sowwy."

That's what he said. Sowwy. He almost laughed, it was that funny. Sorry. He'd meant to say sorry.

"What?"

"Didn't wanna . . ." *hurt you.* Didn't want to hurt you. But those were the rules. She'd been in the way. He'd simply taken control of the situation.

He heard her exclamation of alarm.

Was something wrong, he wondered, as his knees buckled and he slipped to the ground, to the snow.

Snow.

It was so . . . *cool.* Not temperature cool, but cool. Like nothing he'd ever experienced.

He's seen pictures of snow, but in his mind, whenever he'd thought about actually touching it, he'd imagined the outdoor temperature to be a comfortable seventy-two degrees.

From the time he'd been a small child and could look out his bedroom window to see the snow-covered peaks of Kilimanjaro, he'd imagined snow feeling refreshing, like a cool dip on a sweltering day.

Nothing had prepared him for the way it deadened him.

Nothing had prepared him for the way it welcomed him.

He let himself sink into it, let it cushion his fall like the outstretched arms of something sacred.

So seductive.

The perfection of the moment was rudely interrupted.

"You have to get up. Otherwise you'll die out here. Do you want to die? Do you?" the irritating voice demanded.

Did he want to die?

What kind of question was that? A tough one.

He rolled to his back. He opened his eyes.

Standing over him was an angel, her eyes glowing with religious fervor.

Did he want to die?

It took him a while, but he was finally able to get his words lined up in a tidy row, finally able to get them to come out his mouth. "I-Is this a trick question?"

The angel frowned at him.

Irritation?

Puzzlement?

He seemed to evoke such emotions in people.

He'd never fit anywhere. That was his problem. The ol' square peg thing.

"How high can you fly with those wings?" he asked her. He really wanted to know. He'd always thought wings were supposed to be made of feathers, but hers were evergreen branches.

Weird.

But nice.

It reminded him of something. "I've got a funny st-story to tell you. One I think y-y-you'll really get a kick out of—"

She pulled at his arm.

Dead weight.

"Get up. *Please* get up."

"I met this guy once. Can't remember his name. Now that I think about it, I never knew it. For the sake of the story, let's just call him Fred, okay? Fred wanted to get a tattoo that said 'Hell's Angels.' But the tattoo guy hadn't made it past third grade so the tattoo ended up saying 'Hell's *Angles*.' Isn't that funny? Just funny as hell?"

"I'm wetting my pants, it's so funny. Now come on. Get up."

Next thing he knew, she was pulling him to his feet with her angel superpowers, until once more he was kind of standing, or rather slumping against the side of the Jeep. She stuck something on his head, some kind of soft cap. She jammed his arms into a coat, pulling it tight in front, zipping the zipper like he was some little kid.

He kinda liked that.

"You're going to walk."

It was a command.

She grabbed the front of his jacket with both hands, pulling him close, glaring at him with those Mediterranean eyes of hers. "Do you hear me?"

He smiled a smile that felt kind of goofy, even to himself. "I like you."

She blinked, her expression making him think of an owl. He'd surprised her. Startled her, actually.

Then she seemed to come back around, turn into her old drill sergeant self again. "Do you understand?" she asked.

He nodded, not understanding at all, having no idea what he'd just agreed to. All he knew was that he liked her, his sweet Siberia. His Max. To the max. Maxed out. "You're maxing me out."

He laughed at that—a sound that once again triggered that alarmed and surprised and puzzled and worried expression on her face.

His sweet Siberia. It made it sound as if he'd known her quite a while. He liked that, too.

He walked.

For her, he walked.

He couldn't feel his legs. He couldn't feel his feet. He couldn't feel his face. But there was suddenly this warm place in his chest, this little tiny glow. An ember. A promise.

Do you want to die?

Yesterday, his answer would have been that he really didn't give a shit. Today, today his response was slightly more positive.

Today he didn't know.

Claire had never worked so hard in her life. Trevor, or Dylan, or whatever the hell his name was, was down more than he was up. Sometimes he would walk with one arm draped across her shoulder, his weight often pressing her to her knees. When that happened, she would brace her legs under her and straighten, bringing him with her.

Sometimes she had to throw his weight off her in order to get up. She didn't like doing that, because then she had to go through getting him upright all over again. Sometimes she couldn't get him upright so she would grab him under his armpits and, walking backward, she would drag him across the snow. It was backbreaking, and she could only tug him in short bursts. It must not have been much fun for him either, because after a time, he would roll to his hands and knees and crawl until he felt ready to try to stand once more.

She bullied him, and cheered him on, and shouted until her throat hurt, not knowing if her words sank in or not. There were a couple of times when she thought about leaving him, when she considered going the rest of the way by herself. Once home, she could rig up something to put him on, some kind of board that could be pulled across the snow, but then she worried that she might not be able to find him again, or that he might wander away while she was gone. Or she might come back and find him dead and frozen. So she kept on cheering and pulling, bullying and tugging.

Dylan had heard about astral projection, but he'd never participated in the phenomenon. Now he could finally say he had. What else could explain the fact that he had no recollection of getting from the Jeep to Max's joint? Suddenly there was her log cabin, rising out of the snow like some kind of heaven, some kind of celestial palace.

Ten feet from her door, he dropped to his knees at the altar.

"Don't stop now," she said, grabbing at his arm, tugging, trying to pull him to his feet.

"Gotta do something. Something important."

It wasn't easy, but he managed to roll to his back so he was lying faceup. Snowflakes fell into his open eyes.

Then he flapped his wings, and flapped his legs, making an angel for the angel.

Eight

Dylan collapsed just inside the door, seeming quite content to stay there.

The first thing Claire did was run to the thermostat and turn up the heat. She normally kept it set at a cool forty-five degrees for the sake of her wallet, but her uninvited guest was going to need more than that.

The second thing she did was dash to the kitchen table, grab the voodoo doll, and pull out the pin that was deeply imbedded in its soft little head. She stuffed the voodoo doll into the top drawer of the antique desk, then ran back to the man who was lying semiconscious on the floor.

She slapped him lightly on the cheek. "Dylan."

No response.

She slapped him again, harder this time.

"Dylan!" Louder this time.

His eyes came open and his hand shot up, fingers wrapping tightly around her wrist. "Nobody hits me."

"I'm sorry."

His eyes closed. His grip relaxed.

"Don't go to sleep!"

"Huh?" he asked groggily, his eyes rolling back in his head. "Shit big headache. Gotta shit big headache."

"I know! I know! Don't go to sleep! Sit up. You've got to sit up. There. That's the way."

He sat up, but then he just kept going, his head moving forward until his chin was resting on his chest.

It was a struggle, but she finally managed to get him out of his jacket. Just what she was afraid of. His shirt was damp. She quickly unbuttoned it, tearing some of the buttons off in the struggle with dead weight and clinging fabric. She tugged at one arm, then the other.

Shivers started moving through him, one after the other. That was good. Shivering was the body's way of trying to get warm. If he weren't shivering at all, that would be bad.

Now what?

Why hadn't she gotten dry clothes first? If she left him by himself, he would fall over. She ended up lowering him to the floor, his bare back against the inside of his jacket. It looked as if he tried to open his eyes, but gave up.

She got to her feet and ran to the bedroom, jerking open drawers and throwing out clothes until she found an oversized sweatshirt and a pair of flannel pajama pants she'd gotten for Anton.

He'd never worn them. Maybe that had been their whole problem. She'd wanted Anton to be flannel when he was really silk.

She ran back to the living room.

Dylan was right where she'd left him, his face pale, dirty, and blood-caked.

She pulled him upright again. Then, with his back braced against her knees, she tugged the gray sweatshirt over his head, coaxing him, cheering him on as she followed with the arms, finally pulling it down to his stomach.

His pants were wet, too.

She had him lie back down—no argument about that. She unbuttoned and unzipped his pants, then, trying not to think too much about what she was doing, she pulled them over his hips, peeling them down his legs.

His boots. She'd forgotten about his boots.

She quickly unlaced them, tugging them off one at a time, dropping them with a thud. She finished peeling off his pants, leaving him wearing the sweatshirt, striped boxer shorts, and gray socks. The socks joined the rest of the clothes. In the back of her mind, she noticed that he had nice feet. A lot of guys had gross feet. Well, to be fair, a lot of women had gross feet. In fact, she wasn't terribly proud of her own size eights.

She felt his underwear. Dry. She hadn't been relishing the thought of pulling off a complete stranger's, not to mention a criminal's, underwear.

She slipped the flannel pants up his legs, instructing him to lift his hips.

He surprised her by complying.

Now to get him to bed.

"Dylan."

She didn't want to tap at his face again.

"Dylan?"

His eyes rolled. He blinked.

"You've got to get up."

"Too sleepy."

"You have to get to bed where you can get warm."

"No."

She got behind him, put her hands under his armpits. Walking backward, she counted: "One, two, three, *pull.*" She moved him two feet. "One, two, three, *pull.*" Another two feet. By the time she got him to the bedroom, she was out of breath and sweating, even in the coolness of the room.

The bed was an antique, which meant the mattress sat higher off the floor than a modern bed. He was going to have to participate with this part of the program.

"Dylan. Stand up. You're going to have to stand up."

He rolled to his knees. It took a couple of minutes and a lot of coaxing, but he finally got to his feet, enough for her to shove him toward the bed, where he fell face-first. She rolled him over. She tugged and pulled until he was finally lying faceup, a pillow under his head, two down comforters over him.

While he slept, Claire dug out her medical book and looked up concussion. It was all there. The headache, dizziness, vomiting. But then there were some more serious symptoms he didn't have, which led her to believe that things weren't as bad as they could have been. Of course it said to seek medical attention, but that was out of the question due to the weather and road conditions, and her damaged Jeep. She was reassured to read that most concussion victims got well on their own, with simple twenty-four- to forty-eight-hour bed rest.

Next she looked up hypothermia.

It said to put a finger in the patient's mouth to check his temperature. No wonder she'd never been interested in becoming a nurse. It was just too damn personal. Why would anybody want to put her finger in the mouth of a complete stranger? She guessed she should be lucky it was his mouth rather than some other part of his anatomy.

She slammed the book shut, got up from the floor where she'd been sitting cross-legged, and went to check on her patient. He looked exactly the same.

She put a finger to his closed mouth.

His lips were cool, but not extremely cool. And *soft*. They were so soft. . . .

She wiggled her finger between his lips, stopping when she hit his teeth. She pulled her finger away. She couldn't do this.

She stood watching him. He hadn't so much as twitched an eyelid.

She tried again, worming her finger past his lips, this time working her way between his teeth to finally touch his tongue. She stopped, her heart racing.

This was ridiculous. She was checking to see if he was hypothermic.

Yes, but it seemed so personal. So *sexual*.

Nonsense!

She moved her finger across his tongue, testing the surface. It was cold in places, warm in others.

He made a noise low in his throat.

She froze.

His tongue moved against her finger.

She tried to pull it away but couldn't.

He was sucking on it.

She felt a sensation deep in the pit of her stomach, an erotic, weird hot flash.

She tugged harder this time, and her finger came free with a popping sound.

She continued to check on him every hour or so, feeling his feet and hands, noting that they were warmer each time. Somewhere around three in the morning, he woke up and seemed halfway coherent.

"Would you like something to eat?" she asked. "Some hot soup?"

"Bathroom . . ."

She hadn't yet thought of that problem. It turned out he'd already regained enough strength to sit up. Then, with her help, he made it to the bathroom. Once there, he seemed fairly steady so she left him by himself.

When he was back in bed, she heated up some tomato soup and brought it to him in a cup. He finished most of it, then fell back to sleep.

Relieved that he seemed to be on the mend, Claire went back to her makeshift bed on the couch, and slept until morning.

Nine

☽

Dylan was too dazed and weak to do much more than lie in bed and eat the food the mothball woman brought him. He sometimes imagined he was living a Stephen King novel, being held hostage by some mad woman.

Her place was nice. No complaints about that.

A two-story log cabin, a little on the dark side because of the wooden walls and wooden floor, but visually warm, if not actually warm.

There was quite a bit of antique furniture. He'd never been able to figure out if he liked old stuff or not. On one hand, it creeped him out because it was old and you couldn't be sure of where it had been. And it smelled. Antique furniture had a musty smell about it that made him feel like gagging. On the other hand, there was something mysterious and cool about not knowing who'd owned it to begin with, about wondering who they were and what they'd been like. One thing for sure, antique furniture gave off weird vibes that new furniture didn't and couldn't.

Claire's bed had to be ancient. The frame was made of welded iron along with a bit of brass for accent. On top of the mattress was some kind of feather pillow thing that he sank into, that just kind of swallowed him.

It felt great.

To someone who'd lived the most minimalistic lifestyle for the past several years, it felt almost sinful.

She had a lot of quilts. And a lot of pottery stuff, with dried flowers and weeds stuck here and there. She must have preferred natural colors, because there was a lot of brown and green around.

The most intriguing thing about her place were the pictures. He didn't know much about art, but he'd guess that most of them were watercolors, with a few acrylics thrown in.

They were *good*. Better than good. At first he thought they were photographs, they were that good. But then as he lay there, contemplating his situation, he realized they were paintings.

Wow.

Yep, Claire's house was welcoming, the way a soft bed was welcoming when you were dog-tired. It was so alien, so totally different from Louisiana and Arizona.

He could stay here, he decided. He could stay a long time.

* * *

On the second day of his visit—or the third day if you counted the night he'd taken Claire hostage—he discovered how many women it took to hold a man against his will.

Just one.

He woke from a deep doze to find himself handcuffed to the bed.

Helluva deal.

He looked up. These weren't your regular cuffs. They were the kind cops used to transport prisoners, wrapping the length of chain around the prisoner's body. Lucky for him, she hadn't done that. Instead, she's taken up some of the slack, then ingeniously padlocked the chain to the railing at the head of the bed, thus allowing him some freedom of movement, but not much.

"Claire!" He jerked his arms, trying to free himself. The handcuffs rattled against the metal railing.

"Claire! Get your ass in here!"

She finally showed up in the doorway, coffee cup in hand, just calm as you please.

He rattled the handcuffs again. "What the hell's this about?"

She didn't come any closer. Instead, leaning against the doorjamb, one wool-clad foot on top of the other, she casually bobbed a tea bag in her coffee cup, as if giving herself time to contemplate her excuse.

What was the name of that book? *Misery*? He hoped to hell she didn't have an ax or a chain-saw around.

"Claire!" It was a warning.

"We have television here in the boonies, believe it or not."

She was wearing an off-white waffled top tucked into a pair of faded, torn jeans. Her dark hair hung loose on either side of her face. He could smell the cold outdoors on her, even from that distance.

"I know who you are," she said.

"You do?" He didn't like the sound of this. He'd worked hard to keep his identity a secret.

"I know all about you. About your crimes. Your prison record. Your *escape*. I know your name isn't Dylan."

Things were beginning to make sense. "My escape. You heard about that?"

She nodded.

He remembered how those bastards had shot at him, like it was open season on humans. Open season on escaped prisoners. "It was strictly white-collar crime," he said. "I swear."

"On the news, they said you were danger-ous. They said not to approach you, to call the police instead."

"Yeah?"

"Yeah."

He had a vague recollection of Claire, pulling at him, tugging at him, yelling and cussing at him in order to get him back to her house. "So, why didn't you just leave me out there, Claire?" he asked softly.

"I value human life."

That was good to know. It could come in handy in the future.

"I'm sorry about the handcuffs, but you're getting stronger. Feeling better. I couldn't take any chances."

"My arms are numb," he said, trying to sound pathetic, trying for a little guilt manipulation. He wasn't afraid that she'd leave him there long. She was a soft touch. She hadn't tried to shoot him. And she'd saved his life.

"I can't feel my fingers."

"Wiggle them."

She was coming across a little tougher than he thought. "How can I wiggle them if I can't feel them?"

She didn't have an answer for that.

"I need a drink of water." She wouldn't be able to refuse a man a drink.

It worked.

She left, then returned with a glass of water. But instead of releasing him, she lifted the glass to his mouth.

He watched her as he drank.

"Sorry," she said as water trickled down his neck and chest. She gave it a cursory wipe with the waffle-weave sleeve of her shirt. Then she put down the empty glass near the bed. She was turning to leave when he came up with another request.

"Do you have a spare toothbrush? I'd like to brush my teeth."

She had to unlock the cuffs this time. She surely wouldn't brush his teeth for him.

He was feeling relatively confident when she brought him a toothbrush and toothpaste, along with a towel and a glass of water.

He glanced up at the cuffs, waiting.

She put some toothpaste on the brush, jammed the brush in his mouth, and stepped back, arms crossed at her waist.

Oh, that was nice. The toothbrush was stuck in his mouth like a sucker. He pushed it around with his tongue. All he managed to do was spread the minty taste.

"Would you mind?" he asked around a mouthful of foaming toothbrush.

She sighed and approached the bed once more. She grabbed the toothbrush, sloshed it up and down against his teeth, banging his gums, then wiped his mouth with the towel.

"I sincerely hope you take better care of your own teeth," he said, still trying to come up with something she wouldn't be willing to do for him.

"I could use a shave," he ventured.

"You look okay to me."

"It itches."

"So?"

She was *a lot* tougher than he thought. "Are you trying to torture me? Or just keep me from getting away? Because it just looks like you're being mean for the sake of being mean."

That did it.

She left.

She wouldn't be back, he decided. At least not for a while.

But she did come back. Right away.

This time she carried a bowl, a can of shaving cream, and a pink disposable razor. He was patiently waiting for her to bring out the key, when she sat down beside him, one hip against his. She shot some shaving cream into her palm, then rubbed it on his face.

He pulled his head back against the pillow. "You can't shave me."

"Why not?"

"I have a heavy beard. It's hard to do. Takes a certain technique."

"I used to shave my boyfriend sometimes."

"He couldn't have had a beard like mine. Nobody has a beard like mine."

"He was French and Greek. He had a heavy beard."

She dipped the razor in the water, lifted the blade to his face, and proceeded to shave him.

"What's his name?"

"Who?"

"The boyfriend."

"Anton."

He let out a loud snort. Shaving cream flew, some of it hitting her in the face.

"Sorry," he mumbled, trying not to smile, failing.

She wiped her face with the towel.

"You missed a spot."

"Where?"

"I'd point, but as you can see, I'm being cruelly held against my will."

She wiped again, almost getting it all this time.

"This boyfriend," he began. "He isn't your boyfriend anymore?"

"No."

"Why? What was wrong with him?"

"He decided to become a gigolo."

That certainly wasn't what he'd expected. "You're kidding, right?"

"He wouldn't call himself one, but that's what he is. He prostituted himself to get a few rungs higher on the social ladder."

She ran the metal blade against his jaw, rinsed it in the bowl, then put it to his face again.

"What can you expect," he said, "with a name like Anton. It was bound to happen."

"What about your name? I don't know what to call you. The news said your name is Trevor."

"What do you see me as?"

She shrugged. "I don't want to play games. I just want to know what to call you."

"I wasn't lying when I said my name was Dylan. It's my given name. Trevor is just— I don't know . . . something I came across once."

"All done." She wiped his face with the same towel she'd used on herself. She was staring at him.

"What?" he asked.

"I didn't cut you. That's a first."

"I wish I could feel it. I always have to feel my face after a good shave."

"Take my word for it. I didn't miss anything."

"I'm very into touching. I'm a sensual person."

"I've heard prison does that." She got to her feet. "I'll be back later to check on you."

Before he could think of anything else to keep her from leaving, she left.

Shit.

He could hear her walking around, probably getting dressed to go outside, something that could take quite a while in this wasteland. Why would anybody live someplace where they couldn't just walk out the door?

The door slammed.

Two minutes later, he heard the ominous sound of a chainsaw.

Ten

Claire sank the chainsaw blade into the trunk of a dead cottonwood that had blown down last fall. Wood chips flew, hitting her goggles, bouncing off the front of her jeans.

Ten minutes later, her boots were full of sawdust.

The handcuffs had come in handy, she had to admit. And what choice did she have? She couldn't risk his getting away. Now that he was feeling better, her plan was to keep him handcuffed while she walked to the nearest neighbor to call the police.

A simple plan. One she was fairly proud of.

It hadn't been easy, getting the handcuffs on him while he slept. It had been downright scary. But luckily, he was a deep sleeper, and the additional length of chain had kept her from having to adjust his position.

The police would come and take him away in their four-wheel-drive Suburban. They would tell her what a great job she'd done. They might even give her a plaque to hang on the wall. Some kind of good citizen award.

The weird thing was, the disturbing thing was, she was beginning to like him.

How sick. Really sick.

It was just that some of the things he'd said and done had really gotten to her. Like the snow angel. And the gun. Sure, he'd jabbed it into the back of her head, but there was a chance he'd known it wasn't loaded.

Quit making excuses for him. He's a criminal.

She finished cutting several pieces from the trunk of the tree, then turned off the chainsaw. Her back ached and her fingers were numb from the vibration. When she'd first started cutting her own wood a couple of years ago, she couldn't lift her arms above her chest when she was done. She'd discovered that strange phenomenon when she'd tried to raise a glass to her mouth and could only get it halfway there. Now using the chainsaw didn't bother her.

With an ax, she split enough wood to last a few days. They said that firewood warmed you three times: when you cut it, when you carried it in, and when you burned it. Truer words were never spoken. Her long-underwear top was soaked with sweat.

She picked up an armload of wood and headed for the house. Inside, she kicked off her boots, hung up her jacket on the peg near the door, and pulled off her damp cap. She was going to have to strip down to nothing and start over with all dry clothes, otherwise she'd be freezing within a half hour.

Before changing, she loaded the stove with enough wood to keep the house warm for a few hours—enough time for her to go to the neighbors and call the police.

The wood was damp. It began to smoke immediately. She hoped it wouldn't go out. If that happened, the house would be cold before she got back. She could turn on the electric heat, but she'd used it too much already.

She quickly closed the airtight door and adjusted the damper. Then she went to check on her prisoner.

"What do you plan to do with me?"

Some women might just keep him.

Cleaned up, the guy wasn't half-bad. Earlier, when she'd finished shaving him, when the intimidating hair had been removed from his face, her knees had gone weak. He was about the handsomest man she'd ever seen. And now, in the daylight, she could see that his eyes were an ever-changing mixture of gray and hazel.

He wasn't wearing underwear. She knew that for a fact. His solution to having no clean underwear was to simply forget about them. After he'd taken a shower last night, he'd left the giveaway pair of striped boxers on the bathroom floor.

Dressed in nothing but his own faded jeans, jeans that Claire had been grudgingly domestic enough to wash, he'd padded barefoot to the bedroom. Later, Claire had managed to dig out an oversized T-shirt of her own for him to put on, but now, with his arms raised above his head, the shirt crept up to reveal a flat abdomen.

Libby was right. Claire had been holed up in the boonies for too long.

With that theme in mind, she said, "Maybe I'll keep you a while before I turn you in." Why was she teasing him? "I have a lot of stuff around here that I could use help with."

"Kind of a bondage thing?" He actually seemed intrigued with the idea. "Come on," he said. "Let's do it. Right now. You can leave the handcuffs on."

"I thought I wasn't your type," she said, backpedaling as fast as she could.

He shrugged. "I'm bored. And it could be an interesting diversion. I thought that's what you mountain people did up here all winter."

She crossed her arms. "Ha, ha."

"You know something?"

"What?"

"I have to go to the bathroom."

She stared.

Was he kidding?

"My whole system didn't shut down just because you have me strung up. Unlock these things." He squirmed. "Hurry."

This was certainly messing up her schedule. "I can't."

"I won't try to get away. You've got my word."

"Weren't you into fraud? Isn't fraud based on lies?"

"Come on, Claire. Have some mercy here."

She left to return with a plastic jar that had originally contained generic peanut butter. Claire remembered what it had once held because Libby'd had a fit when she spotted it in the cupboard, claiming that the inferior peanuts used in the generic product contained more carcinogens.

Claire placed the jar on the bed beside him. "Use that."

"With my hands bound?"

She really wasn't sure how he was going to go about it. "You can probably figure something out."

"You can either do the honors for me, or unhook my hands."

"I brushed your teeth and shaved you, but I'm not going to help you pee."

"Then come on. Unlock me. One hand. Just one hand. The other one will still be locked. I won't be able to get away with one hand still in cuffs."

She chewed her bottom lip, thinking. If she unlocked the cuff, he might try to grab her. If he grabbed her, he could get the key. But if she moved fast enough, if she unlocked it and jumped away, out of his reach . . .

"This is inhumane."

He was right.

"They wouldn't treat a prisoner like this."

He was right.

"What's it going to be next? Water torture? Bamboo shoots under my fingernails?"

"I'll unlock one hand, but just one."

"That's all I need."

She had the advantage. She hadn't had a concussion or whatever his problem had been. She hadn't almost died in a blizzard. Plus his circulation couldn't be good with his hands above his head like that. His reflexes would be slow. She could move faster. And that's all it would take: speed.

She slipped the key from the front pocket of her jeans and crossed the room. With her left hand, she twisted the cuff, so the lock was exposed, all the while aware that he was staring at her. She stuck the key in the hole. Then, prepared to jump away, she turned the key.

He was so fast she didn't even have a chance to move, or a chance to take a breath, or a chance to fully comprehend what was happening.

The only thing she realized was that he'd gotten the better of her.

One moment, she was turning the key in the lock, the next his fingers were wrapped around her wrist.

He smiled at her in the most alarming, self-satisfied way.

"Well," he said, smiling, smiling. The guy had a hundred smiles in him. A million smiles.

"You're fast," was the only thing she could think of to say.

"No," he said, continuing to smile. "You're just slow."

He was holding her left hand. The key was in her right.

She smiled back.

And gave the key a toss.

The key sailed through the open door, landing with a *ping* somewhere out of sight.

"Now you have to let me go so I can get the key," she told him, her face just inches from his.

Why was he still smiling?

She had the advantage. She had the upper hand.

Didn't she?

He just kept smiling, perfect white teeth in a perfectly handsome face.

She heard the click of the handcuff at the same time she felt metal, still warm from his body, latch around her wrist.

"You know what this is called?" he asked calmly, and, just perhaps, sensually.

"W-What?" she asked, stupefied by the boldness of his idiocy.

"Leveling the playing field."

"But I never wanted to play in the first place."

"Oh, I think you did."

Eleven

"How can you do this to me?" Claire demanded. "I saved your life."

"Just goes to show that you should stop while you're ahead. You messed up twice. Once when you rescued me, and again when you unlocked the handcuffs."

"Are you saying I should have left you out there to freeze to death?"

"I've heard it's not a bad way to go. Rather pleasant after you get past the cold part."

"You're crazy."

"Was there ever any doubt?"

No.

He stared at her, his eyes moving from her face, roaming down her body to come back to where her breasts were pressed against the nubbly cloth of her shirt. He brought up a hand to cup the weight of her breast.

She froze.

"If we're going to die here together, we may

as well have a little fun before we get too weak to enjoy ourselves."

"Don't. Don't do this."

His eyes were just inches from hers. She could see the intricate patterns in his irises, see the dilation of his pupils.

Outside, tires crunched over cold snow.

His pupils shrank.

Car doors slammed.

Footsteps.

Voices.

Claire opened her mouth to shout.

Dylan jerked her down on top of him, pushing her face into the crook of neck. "Shh," he warned, his hand tight against the back of her head. "Not a word."

She could feel his fingers against her skin, feel the threatening pressure of his fingertips.

Minutes passed. There was another sound. Then voices, too far off to hear what they were saying.

More footsteps.

Someone was walking around the house. Just outside the bedroom window, Hallie barked a friendly greeting to the visitors.

Minutes passed.

Then Claire heard the sound of car doors, heard the sound of a vehicle moving away.

Dylan released her.

She let out her breath, her body going limp against his.

"That may have been our only way out of this mess," she said. "It could be weeks, months before anybody comes back. God. We'll both rot here."

It was obvious to Dylan that she was trying to sound tough, but she wasn't having much luck keeping her voice steady.

Now that the danger was over, he became aware of the way her body was sprawled across him, aware of the soft weight of her, the way her breasts were crushed to his chest. He could feel her hipbones beneath the fabric of her jeans. Her legs were tangled up with his, so that she was riding his thigh.

He'd been half-teasing her earlier about having some fun before they died. She wasn't his type. Not that he knew what his type was.

But now, with Claire sprawled across him, her body pressed so sweetly to his, her eyes flashing just inches from his face, her lips red, as if he'd just spent a good ten minutes kissing her, he felt himself harden.

She must have felt it, too, because her eyes widened. First in awareness, then alarm.

He smiled and slid his hand down her back to cup her bottom. Her body was hard, from physical labor, but soft at the same time.

Without taking his eyes from hers, he lifted his hips in a suggestive movement.

Her eyes widened even more, but this time not in alarm but panic.

He sighed and removed his hand from her bottom. They wouldn't be doing anything interesting to pass the time.

He closed his eyes and let his head fall back, waiting for his heartbeat to slow, waiting for his breathing to return to normal.

She maneuvered so she was lying beside him on her back, staring up at the ceiling. "You know how to pick a lock, right? That's the first thing you guys learn, isn't it?"

"I think I was absent the day they were teaching lock-picking 101 at the UPC."

"UPC?"

"University of Petty Crime— What's this in your hair?" He pulled out a wood shaving. "Been playing in the hamster cage again?"

"This isn't the time to joke around. If you don't know how to get these cuffs off, we're in big trouble."

This was nothing. He'd been in big trouble all his life. The last couple of years had been boring as hell. He'd needed something like this. He loved a challenge. And at the moment, he didn't know which was going to be more of a challenge. Getting out of the handcuffs, or wooing Claire.

He had the feeling it would be wooing Claire.

Twelve

☽

It seemed impossible that just days ago Claire had been sitting in The Brewery, bemoaning the dullness of her life. Now here she was, handcuffed to a felon, both of them lying side by side in her bed, staring at the ceiling.

Good times.

It would have been funny if the situation weren't so serious.

"I take it you really didn't have to go to the bathroom," she said, the jar she'd given him earlier pressing against her hip, reminding her of her own weak bladder.

"That's not to say we won't be needing it before we get out of here," he said.

What a lovely idea. One she wouldn't allow herself to linger on. There was no way she would pee in a jar in front of this guy.

Winter days in the mountains were short. Daylight was already fading. In another hour, it would be dark. "I wasn't kidding when I said we could both rot here. If those men come back, we'd better thank God and scream as loudly as we can."

"I thought this might be an opportunity for us to get to know each other. You're always rushing in and out, never sticking around long enough for us to talk."

"This is a game to you, isn't it?"

"Everything's a game. Life's a game."

"Is that how you justify the bad things you do? By telling yourself it's nothing but a game?" A shiver ran through her.

"Cold?"

"Yes, I'm cold! My clothes are damp from sweat. The fire is dying—and I'm freezing!"

With his free hand, he felt the neckline of her shirt. "You'd better get out of that."

"Yeah. Right."

She would no more strip in front of him than pee in front of him.

"Here."

Using his foot, he flipped the quilt close enough to grab it with his hand. He pulled it up over them both, tucking it around their bodies. "There. Isn't this cozy?"

They lay there in silence for a while, with Dylan perusing a stack of books on the bedside dresser. "How about some reading?" he asked. "What have we got here? Let's see . . . *Gardening Made Easy. Passive Solar Heat.* Ah, what's this?" He pulled out a small paperback. "*The Art of*

Extended Orgasm. Hmm. This looks interesting."

"Give me that!" She tried to grab the book from him, but he lifted it out of her reach.

Until then, she'd forgotten she even owned such a thing. It was an irritating gift presented to her by Anton, most likely to make her feel ineffectual in the lovemaking department. When she'd asked him why he'd given it to her, he told her it might teach her a few new tricks. Tricks! He'd called them tricks!

With one hand, Dylan fingered open the book. "Targeting the body's most erotic parts," he read, holding it at the top, his wrist against the spine. "The best strokes, pressures, speeds, and much, much more. How about if I read you a little bedtime story? Let's check out chapter six, 'The Erotic Kiss.' Wonder what that's all about?"

Claire had had enough. She tossed off the blanket, and jumped to her feet.

"Get up," she commanded.

He just lay there looking at her, one leg bent, as if perfectly content to stay where he was for the rest of his life—which could be of short duration if they didn't figure something out. The arm with the book had relaxed so that his wrist was resting against his bent knee. She reached out and jerked the book from his limp fingers, then tossed it across the room where it hit the wall and fell to the floor.

"Get up!" she repeated. "I'm not staying in this bed with you another second."

She shoved at his thigh, urging him to get to his feet. For someone who'd taken her hostage, who'd tied her up and was running from the law, he certainly didn't seem very Type A. He seemed more a sitting-under-a-tree, chewing-on-a-blade-of-grass-while-the-world-went-by type of person.

He swung his feet to the floor. "I thought we were getting nice and cozy here," he griped. "I don't know what you're suddenly in such a hurry for."

"I want to change clothes, and *I* have to go to the bathroom. So get up. We're going to pull the bed across the room. Maybe one of us can reach the key from the door."

"Lemme sit here a minute." He rubbed his shaved face. "Get my bearings."

Maybe it was due to the room's increasing darkness, but now that he was upright, he didn't look so good.

She waited while he sat there, her left hand linked through the bed rail, his right.

"Who's Olivia?"

Had the last ray of sunlight dropped below the horizon? It suddenly seemed as if the lights had gone out, as if any color he'd regained had drained from his face.

"W-What?"

"Olivia."

She was staring at his arm, at the strange tattoo. Now, with it just inches from her face, she could see that below what looked like a horse were the words OLIVIA FOREVER, written in ornate letters. "Your tattoo says 'Olivia'."

His gaze dropped past her inquiring eyes to fall on his ink-stained flesh. He stared at it for a long while, as if he'd never seen it before or had forgotten it was there.

In fact, he seemed to have forgotten that she'd asked him a question until he looked up to see that she was still waiting for an answer.

"It's just a name."

"Nobody has just any name tattooed on his arm."

Dylan had been enjoying himself until Claire mentioned the tattoo. Why didn't she let it go? His flip answer diminished what Olivia had been to him, but he couldn't talk about Olivia. Not to this woman. Not to anybody. And anyway, no words could convey what she'd meant to him. No words could convey the hole her absence had left in his life. No words could convey the depths of his pain.

"She was someone you loved," Claire said, her perception catching him completely off guard.

"Yes."

"But she moved on."

"You could say that," he said, playing for time, stunned by the direction the conversation had taken. How was it this woman with her mothball smell had gone straight to his ache, straight to his hurt. He laughed, trying hard for bitterness. He looked past her. "Don't mention her again."

"What happened? Did she dump you?"

She was pissing him off. She was really pissing him off.

"I wouldn't blame her if she had. You being a criminal and all."

"Shut up," he warned, his voice level and low.

"I wouldn't want to have a relationship with a criminal. I can't imagine going out with someone, let alone being touched and kissed and made love to by someone who'd done bad things."

She was egging him on. She was doing this on purpose. An age-old frustration pumped through his veins. "Can't you?"

She stood in front of him, one leg brushing against his knee. There was a smug expression on her face, one that said that they might have both been trapped, but she had the upper hand. She had stumbled upon his weak spot, his Achilles' heel.

"Don't you know any better than to tease a trapped animal?"

He wrapped his legs around hers and grasped her arm with his free hand, supremely satisfied to see the smugness in her eyes replaced by fear. He pulled her down on top of him, keeping his legs wrapped around hers, his thighs pressing her into his groin. He released her just long enough to shift his hand from her arm to the back of her neck. "You have no idea what it feels like to be kissed by a criminal? That sounded like an invitation, Max. Was that supposed to be an invitation?"

"Don't call me that." She squirmed in his grip, shoving against his chest with her one free hand.

He laughed at the futility of her struggle. "Is this the way you like it, Max? Are you into bondage?" With his hand splayed against the back of her neck, he brought her closer, her mouth just inches from his. He lifted his head, lifted his face to meet hers. He heard her soft indrawn breath, saw her eyelids flutter closed. Saw her full lips tremble in the sweetest of invitations. And then, just as his lips brushed hers, she spoke one word.

"Olivia."

Like someone stung, he released his hold on the back of her neck. Her eyes flew open and she pushed away from him, as much as she could with her hips still crushed between his thighs.

He let out a cry of frustrated anger. "Damn you! How can you do this? You don't even know me. You don't know anything about me. And yet you *do*. You know everything about me. Are you a psychic? Are you reading my mind right now?"

She squirmed against him, shoving at his chest with one small hand.

"Come on. Tell me what I'm thinking."

"No."

"I'm thinking that you feel good. Really good."

"Do you want to know what *I'm* thinking?"

"Not particularly."

Anger flared in her eyes. "I'm thinking how lucky Olivia was to get rid of you."

He unwrapped his legs from hers and shoved her away from him. Feeling mad enough to move the whole damn house, he got to his feet and pulled, not caring if the cuffs cut into his wrist.

He dragged the bed across the floor. The woman—Claire—walked backward, trying to move fast enough to stay out of his way. "Slow down!" she gasped when the bed collided with her for the second time.

"Get out of the way!" He pulled until the bed built up enough momentum to slam into the open doorway, almost pinning Claire to the wall.

"Whew."

She stared up at him in surprise and more than a little fear. "I'd get that removed if I were you," she said, indicating the tattoo.

He smiled a completely joyless smile. "It's the only thing that keeps me going."

"And I thought you hadn't exhibited many Type A traits. You sure made up for it fast."

"Can you see the key?" he asked.

She twisted around. "No."

"Here. Get your feet off the floor."

She tucked her feet under her bottom as he spun the bed around so the head was near the door.

"I see it," he said. "Give me that blanket."

Keeping a grip on one corner of the blanket, he gave it a toss, dragging the quilt across the floor and back to him.

On the fourth try, Claire heard the soft *ping* of metal. Dylan pulled the blanket closer, then bent over and picked up the key.

He unlocked his cuff, then looked up at Claire, who was kneeling on the edge of the bed waiting.

She held out her hand. "The key."

His eyebrows lifted.

"Come on," she said in disbelief. "You're not going to leave me here. You can't."

"It might be fun."

"For you."

"Exactly."

"Give me the key."

"I'll brush your teeth. I'll shave you. Do you have any places that need to be shaved?" His gaze traveled slowly down her body, then back up to make sensual contact with her eyes.

"Yeah, my back."

His mouth dropped open, then he let out a shout of laughter. Hand to his stomach, he doubled over, unable to stop laughing.

She frowned. Her intent had been to disgust him, not set him off in an orgasm of mirth. "You can stop laughing now."

He finally started to wind down, actually reaching that period where you stop laughing completely, then start again, then stop until the whole thing finally fizzles out.

A shiver ran through her. It was so cold! The temperature in the room had to have dropped twenty degrees during their little intimacy session.

With a smile still hovering at the edges of his mouth, he reached over—and unlocked the cuff.

Her hand fell away from the bed rail, her arm too weak to do anything but drop to the mattress. With her other hand, she rubbed her wrist, trying to get some of the feeling back in it. Then she scrambled off the bed and ran for the bathroom. The lock was broken so she only pretended to secure the door behind her, hoping he would leave her alone.

Thirteen

Back to square one, she thought, peeling off clothes that were almost dry. Not bothering with a bra, she grabbed a flannel shirt from the hook on the back of the door and slipped it on. But when she tried to button it, she couldn't make her left hand work.

Two minutes later she was still struggling.

Dylan knocked on the door. "Hurry up."

"I am, I am."

She was still working on button number two. *Damn.* It was next to impossible with only one hand.

The doorknob turned and he walked right in.

"Here. Move your hands."

"I can do it."

"I'm standing right here."

"I don't want your help."

"For chrissake." He brushed her hand away.

She watched as he buttoned her shirt, all the while aware of her nakedness under the soft flannel. There had been a moment back there when she had wanted him to kiss her. And even now, the thought of such a kiss scared her. But it also intrigued her. She kept wondering what his mouth would feel like pressed to hers.

"What's a girl like you doing with a set of handcuffs?" he asked, his head bent in studious concentration.

"You mean someone who smells like moth-balls and drinks castor oil?"

"No, I mean someone who lives in the mountains by herself and chops her own fire-wood." He actually sounded curious about her, wonder of wonders. Maybe she wasn't quite as boring as she thought.

"They were a present."

"From Anton?"

"Maybe." It was none of his business.

Was it her imagination, or did his hands linger over the last button?

When he was finished, he ran his fingers down the entire row, starting just below her chin and ending above her belly. "There," he said looking up, his hand still on her stomach.

"Thanks."

"Anytime."

They were standing in the tiny bathroom, face to face, toe to toe.

She inched past him, her heart racing. She didn't look back, but she knew he was watching her.

In the living room, she discovered that he'd loaded the stove with wood. From the bathroom came the sound of the shower.

Still cold, Claire slipped on her down jacket and crocheted cap. She fed Hallie, then put a kettle of water on the stove and waited for the room to warm up. Whenever she was really cold, she went outside to the sauna. It used electric heat, and took only a short while to warm up. But lately she'd been trying to conserve on the electricity, plus she didn't think her relationship with the criminal had moved to sharing a sauna, and somehow she thought he would probably follow her there.

A few minutes later, she heard him in the bedroom, shoving the bed back where it had been. Maybe it was because she was exhausted, but the whole handcuff thing seemed so stupid now. The guy was harmless. Was it really her duty to be a good citizen and turn him in? Shit, she didn't know. She just wondered who Olivia was.

Five minutes later, she was curled up in the corner of the couch in front of the stove, a cup of hot chocolate in her hands.

Behind her, he opened the front door, letting in a blast of arctic air. He whistled.

Hallie made an instant appearance, slobbering all over Dylan, her nails tapping on the wooden floor as she danced around in excitement.

Dylan good-doggied her and pet her hard,

the way guys did when they roughhoused with dogs. Claire didn't think Anton had ever given Hallie a single pat on the head.

"There's water for hot chocolate on the stove," she said over her shoulder.

She heard him banging around in the kitchen. A few minutes later, he sat down on the floor near the fire, his back against the couch. Hallie dropped down beside him, her head resting on his thigh.

"How much trouble can you get into if the police catch you?" Claire asked.

He ruffled the thick hair around Hallie's neck. Claire noticed that Dylan's wrist was red and raw-looking from his angry tug at the bed.

"I don't know."

She swallowed. "A life sentence?" She could barely get the question past her tight throat.

"I don't know."

The room was getting almost hot. Claire suddenly remembered her jacket and cap. She took them off.

"That's the ugliest damn thing I've ever seen in my life," he said, staring at the cap with the same horrified expression Libby often used.

"I like it."

"*Why?*"

"Because it was a present. Because someone went to the trouble to make it for me."

The heat, after the cold, was making them both drowsy.

Ten minutes later, Claire was half-asleep in one corner of the couch. She opened her eyes once to see Dylan sprawled out in front of the fire.

She didn't know another thing until pounding at the front door had her sitting upright, her heart hammering in alarm the way it always did whenever something awakened her from a deep sleep. Hallie ran to the door, barking.

Claire was surprised to see that it was light out.

She checked the wall clock—6:45 A.M.

Knock, knock.

"Claire!" It was a man's voice.

On the floor near her feet, Dylan stirred. His eyes came open to stare at her.

Scared.

Don't say anything.

Please.

"Just a minute!" Claire shouted, rubbing her face, getting to her feet.

She sneezed violently. Once. Twice. Behind her, she heard the sound of Dylan scrambling across the floor, getting the hell out of there.

She opened the door just in time for another sneeze. "Sorry," she mumbled behind her hand, eyes watering.

Sheriff Docherty.

Hallie gave him a welcome of her own, the usual crotch sniff.

"Hallie." Claire pulled her away.

"I stopped by yesterday and nobody was

home. Then this morning we found your Jeep. You okay?"

"Fine." She sniffled. "Except for a cold."

Hallie wandered a few feet away, then squatted in a pile of snow. Poor girl had a weak bladder.

"I don't want to scare you, but you probably heard there is a criminal loose. You sure everything is okay?"

Claire looked down at the bucket of frozen vomit Dylan had left at the door. She looked back up. "Fine."

"Haven't seen anything, have you?" he asked, watching her intently. All she would have to do was nod, or mouth the word Help. He wasn't slow. He would understand.

"Like I said, I have a cold. I've been holed up here, trying to get over it. I was probably asleep when you stopped by yesterday. That cold medicine really knocks me out."

"If you see or hear anything, get in touch with me, okay?"

She gave him a rough smile. She'd always suspected that Sheriff Docherty kind of liked her. Seeing her at this time of day would cure him of that. She felt kind of sorry for him. Nothing worse than a shattered dream.

Fourteen

Dylan stood wedged into a corner of the loft, heart hammering, his breathing ragged.

He listened to the sound of Claire's voice, waiting to hear the policeman's surprised shout. Waiting to hear heavy footfalls. Waiting to have a gun pointed at him. Instead, he heard Claire telling the person at the door that she had a cold. Then, instead of telling him that Dylan had stolen her Jeep, she said that she herself had run into the tree.

Dylan strained to hear the rest of the conversation.

"Could you do me a favor and call a tow truck?" she asked.

"You should get a phone," the man answered in a concerned voice. He liked her. Dylan could hear it in the guy's voice. Kind of a shy respect, but also frustration. He wanted her to be safe, but it wasn't his place to say too much.

He said his good-byes. The door slammed.

Dylan listened to the fading sound of the police vehicle. Then he collapsed to the floor. A minute later, he rolled to his back, a bent hand to his chest. That was close. Son of a bitch.

Little by little, he began to relax. Little by little, he began to take note of his surroundings.

An artist's studio. The loft was an artist's studio. There were a couple of worktables, two easels, flood lights, tubes of paints—watercolors, not oils or acrylics. Bottles of artist's ink. Brushes, pens, mat boards, sketchpads, rags.

Slowly, he got to his feet and moved to the center of the room where the skylight dropped a rectangle of sunshine on the wooden floor.

He'd found himself wondering what Claire did for a living, speculating about the possibility of her being a musician, or maybe a writer. So . . . Claire was an artist. She had painted the pictures he'd seen downstairs.

How strange . . .

His thoughts went back to another time, to another artist he had known in another life, a friend who had blended his dreams in pastels on public sidewalks. That was so long ago. . . .

Dylan picked up a paint tube. Mars Violet. He put it down and picked up another. Hooker's Green. He smiled to himself. Rose Madder. Raw Umber. What great names. Cool names. He'd always loved paint names.

He heard footsteps on the ladder. He didn't turn. He put down the tube of paint and approached the worktable where ten to twelve pictures, some finished, some not, were strewn.

She liked birds. No, she *loved* birds. But there were other things, too. Flowers. Frogs. Doorways with vines. Trees. Grasshoppers.

He picked up a watercolor of a grasshopper. It was so damn *detailed*. He hadn't known grasshoppers had all those dots along their legs. He hadn't known they were such a miracle.

"He's gone."

"Mmm?"

"The policeman. He's gone."

Dylan was so absorbed in her paintings that he'd forgotten all about the person at the door.

He turned. "Are all of these yours?" he asked, even though he knew the answer.

She crossed the room, walking under the shaft of sunlight and beyond to stand at the table next to him. "I'm putting together a proposal for a card company." She shifted the pictures around, uncovering one miracle after the other, then just as quickly covering them back up, as if she couldn't bear to look at her own work. "People always say my drawings are too exact. That they lack imagination." She sounded frustrated and dissatisfied with what she had created, obviously not seeing what he saw.

"Who told you that? The same people who look at a pile of twisted metal and call it art?"

"Maybe that pile of twisted metal *is* art. Maybe the whole idea of art is to create something new, not duplicate what's already there."

"You aren't duplicating. You're showing me what I missed, what I never took the time to notice. You're helping me to see things with clearer eyes."

She looked at him for a long moment, as if trying to decide if he was feeding her a line.

"Why'd you do that?" he asked.

"What?"

"Not tell the cop I was here." Had she been scared that he'd do something drastic that might hurt her, or hurt the cop?

"I didn't want to get you into any more trouble than you're already in. I didn't want them to find out that you'd abducted me."

That surprised him. Surprised the hell out of him. "I wish I could do something for you in return."

"Like what?"

"I don't know. Knit you a goofy-ass hat maybe, but I don't know how to knit."

"If you just turn yourself in, they would go easier on you; you know that."

He ignored her. Instead, he took both of her hands and slowly lifted them to his mouth.

"Don't." She tried to pull her hands away, but he wouldn't let her. "My hands are so ugly."

"They're beautiful." He kissed one set of raw, dry knuckles at a time. "Take good care of these babies."

Fifteen

☾

"You've never killed anybody, have you?"

Claire's nose was stuffy, so her question came out more like, "You've nebber killed anybuddy, hab you?"

She was propped up in bed, a pile of quilts over her, reeking of cough drops, and Vicks VapoRub, a mound of rumpled tissues on the bed and floor.

"No."

She believed him. Did she believe him simply because she *wanted* to?

Yes.

That was never a good reason to believe somebody.

He sat down on the edge of the bed. "There are limits to what I'll do."

"You'd better stay back. You don't want to catch this."

"I have a strong immune system."

"Nobody has a strong enough system to keep from getting this cold. It's bad. Really bad."

"I've never had a cold."

Having a cold always dropped her IQ about twenty points, but no way was she falling for such a whopper. "Everybody gets colds."

He blandly lifted his eyebrows, as if to say she could believe him if she wanted to. It didn't make any difference to him.

"I've got to get up." She tossed the covers, tissues flying, but she didn't make a move to get out of bed.

Dylan covered her again. "Stay in bed. I'll cut some wood and do whatever else needs to be done."

"Hallie. Hallie needs to be fed."

"I'll take care of it."

She let her head fall back against the pillow, thinking, I could get used to this.

Trying to be as quiet as possible, Dylan tore a piece of duct tape from the roll, then smoothed it across the rip in his jacket where the down was coming out. Then he put on the jacket, feathers flying. He blew, trying to keep them away from his face. He'd found a wool cap in a wooden box by the door. He slapped it on his head, curving the bill the way he liked it. Nothing worse than a flat bill. He shrugged into Claire's backpack, the straps adjusted to accommodate his larger frame. One last thing.

Before leaving, he opened her purse and pulled out her wallet. Three hundred bucks. What was she doing going around with three hundred bucks in her purse?

Trying not to think about what he was doing, he stuffed all but fifty dollars deep in the front pocket of his jeans and headed out the door.

He took off, sticking to the tracks left by the cop's vehicle. He hadn't made it to the end of the lane when he realized Hallie was following him.

"Stay," he commanded, nervously looking back at the house.

Hallie just wagged her tail and jumped on him, leaving a couple of huge paw prints on the front of his jacket. "Dumb dog. I don't think Claire would appreciate it if I took you, too."

He felt bad enough leaving the way he was, he didn't need Hallie's reproach to drive home his betrayal. But this might be his only chance, and it wasn't like he was going keep her money. He'd pay her back as soon as he got someplace safe where he could put in a call to Zeke, the brain behind Dylan's financial dealings. Wouldn't Zeke be surprised to hear from him? Good ol' Zeke. He'd taken care of everything while Dylan had been away.

He headed back to the house, Hallie at his heels. He opened the door and silently motioned for her to go inside. Instead she sat there smiling up at him. "Go on," he whispered, motioning with his hand again. She just sat there.

He shoved her, pushing at her rump with both hands. Once she was inside, he quickly shut the door, turned, and ran.

Claire woke up to the sound of Hallie scratching at the door to get out.

"Dylan?"

Scratch, scratch, scratch.

It was getting dark. Where was Dylan?

She tossed back the covers and got out of bed, the floor cold as ice on the bottom of her feet. Where were her socks? She couldn't find her socks.

"Dylan?"

Scratch, scratch, scratch.

"I'm coming, Hallie."

Hallie whined that high-pitched excited whine she used when she thought she'd found something really great like a dead squirrel.

Claire went to the door and let her out, quickly shutting the door behind her. Outside, Hallie took off around the house, barking.

Idiot dog.

Bleary-eyed, her head feeling as big as a watermelon, Claire turned around, intending to drag herself directly back to bed, when she stopped.

In the middle of the kitchen table was her purse. And beside her purse, was her open wallet. She picked it up and looked inside. Two twenties and a ten.

The son of a bitch had taken most of her rent money.

You just lie there and rest. Ol' Daddy Dylan will take care of everything.

Grrr! She could pull out her own hair. How could she have been so stupid? So blind?

He'd taken care of everything all right. Now what was she going to do? There was a shop in town where she sold her artwork on commission, but winter was the slow season, the *really* slow season. So slow that she rarely sold anything from the beginning of January until tourist season started toward the end of May.

Damn.

The antique furniture wasn't hers. The only thing of value she owned was her Jeep, and it wouldn't be worth much now with the crumpled front end. She would have to see if she could pay her rent a little late. Maybe she could sell a picture somewhere.

Damn.

Claire's cold lasted a week. During that time Libby came by and gave her a ride into town to pick up her Jeep. On the way there, Claire almost told Libby about Dylan. "You know those handcuffs you gave me?" she began.

"Use 'em yet?" Libby asked in a tone that said she knew she hadn't. "How about that voodoo doll? Did you put some of Anton's hair on it?"

"Anton? No . . ." Claire said vaguely. "I haven't done that." She couldn't bring herself to tell Libby about her abduction. Libby may have been a good friend, but she also loved passing on a juicy story. The weird thing was, Claire didn't think of it as an abduction. And even though he'd robbed her and smashed up her Jeep, leaving her with a repair bill she wouldn't be able to pay, when she looked back on the whole thing it was like recalling an adventure. And now, with that adventure behind her, it didn't even seem real.

She would catch herself daydreaming about him, and she would have to remind herself that the guy was a loser, an even bigger loser than Anton, who before Dylan had come along had been King of the Losers. So why hadn't she turned him in?

She'd heard the police were no longer looking for him. That made her even more aware of her negligence in the law-abiding citizen department. She'd never done anything illegal in her life, except for an occasional U-turn.

Of course, there had been that time she'd accidentally gotten stoned. How was she supposed to know that Magic Muffins meant the little goodies had pot in them? She just thought it meant they were made from some super-duper recipe. They'd been super-duper all right.

"I still don't get what you were doing out during that blizzard," Libby said, bringing Claire back to the present. "You really need to get a phone, Claire. I mean it. At least a cellular phone for emergencies."

"You're right." But that didn't mean Claire had any intention of getting one, not in the near future anyway, not when she didn't even have money for rent, thanks to her brief moment of misplaced compassion.

After picking up her Jeep and returning home, Claire came across the voodoo doll with Dylan's hair still glued to it. She stared at it for a long time. She picked up a black pin. Then she put it down, turned the doll over to the good voodoo side, picked up a white pin, and stuck it in the chest.

Dylan lay fully clothed on the bed of the hotel room with its orange spread and matching curtains, hands behind his head, watching an old episode of *Kids in the Hall.*

When the skit ended, Dylan reluctantly changed channels. He should be watching the news to see if his disappearance was still a big deal. Claire had surely turned him in by now.

He didn't have to channel-surf long before he came upon an interview with the guy who'd walked away from the plane crash, the chess player, Daniel French.

He was talking about how bad Dylan had looked when he'd last seen him.

"Do you think he could have walked to safety?" the interviewer asked.

The man thought a moment, then slowly shook his head. "I seriously doubt it. He couldn't have gone far on his own. And then with that storm . . . I'm afraid he's buried out there under ten feet of snow and nobody's going to find him until spring."

The interviewer thanked the man, then turned back to the camera. "There you have it. An opinion that has been echoed around here for the past three days. The search has been called off. Every day that goes by has officials more convinced that the mysterious man going by a string of aliases has chosen a false name for the last time. Back to you, John."

"How will anyone know what name to put on the death certificate?" John asked with that forced time-to-toss-in-a-joke voice.

"I don't know," the correspondent on location said, unable to come up with a reply, probably pissed that good ol' John had made him look stupid.

Dead.

Being presumed dead was something Dylan had always fantasized about. What better way to start over? He clicked off the television, pulled the phone off the dresser to rest it on his stomach, and put in a call to New Orleans. He needed money. Maybe a new identity. Zeke could get him both those things.

He had another thought. Claire hadn't turned him in. He wished he could thank her for that. He really did.

Zeke was surprised and pleased to hear from him all right.

"I figured you were hiding out somewhere, just waiting for things to cool down," Zeke said.

They bullshitted for a little while, then Dylan said, "Zeke, I need you to send me some cash."

"No problem. What about a fake driver's license and credit cards?"

"That, too."

Dylan gave him the motel name and address. "Whose name do I put on it?"

Dylan thought a moment. "Charles Black."

After hanging up, Dylan lay back in bed, hands behind his head, and stared up at the ceiling. Talking to Zeke had reminded him of the old days. His mind spun backward, to a time when life had been more magic than hardship. . . .

Early childhood for Dylan had been a series of new and exciting locations. His parents were missionaries, moving from place to place, country to country, living in one poor village after another. He and his sister, Olivia, had ridden camels in Sudan. In Ethiopia, their classroom was nothing more than a thatched roof above a dirt floor, their beds made of the same woven material that kept out the sun and heat. Dylan had seen the highest mountain in the world, and he'd waded in the very sea Moses had parted. His heart had been stolen by a little girl in

Madagascar who wore beaded gowns and carried a lemur on her shoulder, the lemur making his hissing cockroach seem pretty insignificant. And even though he was too young to understand the unrest in South Africa, he felt the injustice of it.

While living in South Africa, he and Olivia would lie in bed at night and listen to their parents talking from the kitchen. Dylan's father, normally a gentle man, a person who had never once raised his voice to his children, would shout in anger, and bang his fist on the table in frustration.

South Africa was the beginning of the end.

One hot night, Dylan was awakened from a deep sleep by a woman's screams. That was followed by a series of popping sounds and angry foreign voices, then the echo of booted feet—men running away.

Heart pounding, feeling sick to his stomach, Dylan left the bedroom and stepped into the narrow hall that led to the kitchen. Under the light of a bare bulb, his parents lay dead, murdered.

He didn't know how long he stood there, unable to move, unable to pull his gaze away from the horror. Behind him, he heard Olivia's groggy voice. "What's wrong?"

"Go back to bed." He turned and pulled her down the hallway to the bedroom, where she went back to sleep and he sat on the end of the bed, waiting for an adult to show up.

Dylan was ten years old.

* * *

He and his sister were taken to the American Embassy by Father Sebastian, a red-faced Irishman who had worked with Dylan's parents. There they followed a long hall to be presented to a man behind a desk in a room that smelled like stale cigars. In one corner, an oscillating fan moved back and forth, clicking every time it reached the end of its sweep.

The man asked them about relatives.

Dylan's father had never spoken about any of his family. "My mother has a brother," Dylan offered. He'd seen him once, and hadn't liked him. The man had been a loud contrast to his father's quiet, almost shy reserve. He drank a lot and called his wife "the little woman." Dylan didn't know what his aunt's real name was.

They had a hard time finding Uncle Hank. It seemed he'd changed his name and moved to Louisiana—"because of a little trouble with the law," as Uncle Hank later put it.

And so Dylan and Olivia found themselves living with their loud, obnoxious uncle and timid aunt. On the day of their arrival in the little Louisiana town of Black Water, his uncle gave Dylan a pat on the head and a pellet gun, telling him to go shoot sparrows. Later, when he was by himself, Dylan poured the pellets out on the ground.

His uncle ran a gas station, Hank's Gator

Stop. SEE THE LIVE ALLIGATOR, a huge painted sign near the road shouted. The alligator was kept in a tank next to the gas station. The tank was so small that the reptile couldn't turn around. Dylan's job was to add fresh water to the tank every day. While Dylan ran the hose over the alligator's spiny back, he would imagine the alligator getting loose and taking out its revenge on Uncle Hank. One day someone turned his uncle in to the Humane Society and some people came and took the alligator away.

"There goes half my income!" Uncle Hank shouted, shaking a fist after the departing truck and gator-filled trailer. He glanced around and saw Dylan standing there.

"What are you smiling about?" He took a swing at him, but Dylan dodged his fist and ran.

Dylan and Olivia were used to new and strange places, but they'd always had their parents for support. Their father's quiet strength had always been there to back them, along with their mother's displays of affection.

There was none of that in the Leary household. After years of emotional abuse, their aunt Doris had turned into a shell of a human, a robot who simply went about her daily chores, ignoring everything that went on around her. Even at a young age, Dylan realized that her withdrawal from the world was the only way she could cope. And yet he couldn't help but resent the way she wouldn't stand up to her husband.

If not for Olivia, Dylan may have killed himself.

Two years after moving to Louisiana, Olivia died. They said it was some exotic disease she'd picked up in Africa, but in Dylan's twelve-year-old mind, he knew sorrow had killed his sister.

With Olivia gone, Dylan's life had no direction, no purpose. She had been by his side most of his life. He couldn't remember a time when she hadn't been there.

It didn't seem possible for hell to get any bleaker, but then Uncle Hank died of a heart attack. Two days after the funeral, Aunt Doris left. She just tossed her bags in the trunk of her car and drove away. Dylan was never sure if she'd left him behind deliberately or not. It was just possible that she'd never known he was there.

This time he was sent to an adoption agency in New Orleans. But it seemed nobody wanted a twelve-year-old with too much history.

Dylan began wandering the streets, playing checkers with some of the old men who hung out in the French Quarter. In New Orleans, he learned to beg for money. In New Orleans, he got dark from the sun and dirty from the streets, until he didn't look any different from the rest of the street people, although once in a while a pretty woman would comment on the intensity of his eyes.

One day when the old men got sick of Dylan beating them at every game of checkers, they shooed him away. He wandered down an alley with the usual voodoo shops and whorehouses. A drunk American staggered out of a red door set back off the alley. Young American guys were always coming to New Orleans to get drunk, get tattoos, and screw the whores. He proudly showed Dylan the tattoo he'd just gotten. Even though Dylan was only twelve, even though he hadn't had much of an education, he knew you didn't spell Hell's Angels that way.

But seeing the tattoo gave him an idea. An idea he couldn't get out of his head. He missed Olivia terribly. But it was getting harder and harder to remember exactly what she looked like, and exactly how she sounded when she talked.

And so he got the idea to play checkers for money. It wasn't long before he'd made enough money to get a tattoo. Until he had enough money to spell "Olivia Forever."

Sixteen

Claire sat curled up on the couch in the corner of the loft, her feet tucked under her, a sketchpad across her bent knees, staring blankly at the wall. She hadn't accomplished anything since Dylan left.

Old doubts plagued her. Were the pictures she'd done so far any good? Good enough to submit? The more she looked at them, the less confident she became. Her drawings weren't bright. Weren't eye-catching. They didn't shout at you.

Too quiet. Too soft. The voices of a million critics came back to haunt her. Maybe they were too real. Too bland.

She'd once had an art teacher who told her she'd never make it unless she changed her style.

But to change . . . If she couldn't express herself in her own way, with her own talent, what was the point? Unwittingly, that teacher had helped Claire see the direction she needed to go.

From that moment, she became a rebel, clinging desperately and perhaps foolishly to her own style, even if it meant never making it, even if it meant that she might eventually crash and burn. Because she would rather crash and burn than become yet another artist suppressing her talent to mimic someone else.

From outside came the sound of Hallie's frantic barking, pulling Claire out of yet another daydream.

She noticed that the light in the room had changed, telling her evening was approaching, telling her she'd wasted one more afternoon.

From downstairs came the sound of the front door opening, then closing. A heavy footfall echoed through the house, carrying upstairs to where Claire sat still as a mouse.

Dylan?

"Claire?"

A male voice. One she thought she recognized.

Heart hammering, Claire put her tablet aside and pushed herself up from the soft depth of the couch. "Anton?"

Two weeks ago, she would have been thrilled to hear his voice. Two weeks ago, she would have hurried down the ladder to greet him. Now she hesitated.

What was he doing here? What did he want?

His footsteps moved in her direction. "Claire?"

She hung back.

She stared at the opening in the floor, watching until Anton's dark head appeared.

"Claire!"

He was tan, very tan, as if he'd recently spent a lot of time on the ocean lounging around on somebody's huge yacht. He flashed his white teeth at her and swung himself free of the ladder.

He wore a black leather jacket that he took off and tossed over the back of a chair. He stood there, smiling, waiting for her to throw herself at him.

Two weeks ago, she would have done just that.

"What are you doing here?" she asked instead.

His clothes were expensive. Dark, kind of shiny. His hair had been styled to perfection. He lifted his arms to her, his head tilted in the sweet little boy way she remembered that said, I'm so charming and handsome that you'll surely forgive anything I've done. Glittering from a ring on his pinky finger was what looked like a diamond. A big one.

She saw no reason to be nice. "When you cross over, you really cross over."

"Claire, I came to see you."

Had he always sounded so affected? Or was it something he'd picked up recently? "Don't you mean, you came here so *I* could see *you*?" she asked.

He didn't get it. That was obvious from the puzzled expression on his face. But he'd never been one to linger overlong on something he didn't understand. He simply moved on. That had been one of the things Claire found fascinating about him—his ability to shrug things off and move on. It was a handy trait.

Looking at him now, she could see that it was just selfishness on his part.

"Come on," he said, arms still outstretched in that look-at-me pose. "No hug? No kiss?"

The new affectations were getting on her nerves. His mannerisms, his way of gesturing and posturing, were enough to make her stomach churn.

"If you've come to get your things, then get them and go."

"Claire, Claire." He shook his head and smiled, as if to say he wasn't falling for this aloof game. He moved toward her. "You want me. You know you want me."

Had he always been such a creep? Had she never seen him for what he really was? No, surely her judgment wasn't that bad. The old Anton had been cocky, but this person in front of her— He was like a cartoon. A caricature of the old Anton.

"Get out of here or I'll call the police."

"You don't have a phone." His savoir faire was fading.

"I got one."

"I know you, Claire. You hate phones. You would never have a phone."

He knows me so well.

In a flash, she understood him. Completely. He hadn't been a master at being the perfect mate. He'd been a master at reading her. And he had fed on her need of him, her adoration of him. Now that he could see she no longer adored him, he was angry. To him, *she* was the traitor.

"You thought you could come back here anytime and I'd be waiting for you, didn't you?"

"Don't play these games, Claire." He grabbed her by both arms. He pulled her close. "You've been waiting for me. I know you. I know how hot you always were for me. That kind of thing doesn't change. You want me. You'll always want me. I'll bet you've been lying in bed at night, all hot and horny, thinking about me." His voice dropped to a whisper. "I know what you like. I know *everything* you like. I know when to go fast, and when to go slow. I know just where to touch you to make you crazy."

"Get out! Now!" She was outraged at him, at herself for allowing him to intrude upon her life to such a point.

In the months they'd been together, he'd never displayed violence. Now anger flared in his eyes. His fingers dug into her arms. "I didn't think you had any surprises left in you." He began shoving her, forcing her backward. "But I had no idea you liked it rough. No idea at all."

He turned her rejection into an open assault, one that demanded his retaliation. Claire knew she should try to placate him, knew she should back off and say the things he wanted to hear, but she had too much self-respect for that. And absolutely no respect left for him.

"Get your hands off me," she said through gritted teeth. "You son of a bitch." There was no fear in her, only anger.

What remained of his mask crumbled completely. There wasn't a remnant of the person Claire had once known.

He took her by surprise, shoving her down to the floor, falling on top of her, holding her with his weight while he struggled with one hand to undo her jeans.

He never could chew gum and walk at the same time. The distraction allowed Claire to bring a hand to his face. She tried to scratch him, but she had no nails. Her pathetic attack only made him madder. He grabbed her hand. Without thought, she bit his arm. He screamed and let go, but before she could put any distance between them, he grabbed her again.

Together, they fell backward, the French easel that had been a gift from her father slid across the floor, shattering when it hit the wall. Claire reached behind her, her hand coming in contact with the other easel. She pulled it down on top of Anton. He tossed it aside, her pictures flying, tearing. She saw his arm moving toward her, saw his hand. She ducked, blocking his blow with her forearm.

For a moment, she felt a sense of power. In the middle of the battle, it occurred to her that they were fairly evenly matched. She'd chopped a lot of wood in her day, and he'd spent a lot of time putting his wood to people.

She was actually thinking she had the upper hand when he tackled her, knocking the air from her lungs. With his added weight as momentum, they slid across the floor. She slammed into the wall, banging her head against the windowsill.

"No," he said, gasping for breath. "I never knew you liked it so wild."

She opened her eyes to see him kneeling over her, fiddling with his pants. Next to her was the dresser where she'd hidden the gun. She rolled to the side, tugged open the bottom drawer and grabbed the gun, shaking it free of the T-shirt. Without hesitation, she pointed the weapon directly at Anton's shocked face.

"You have no idea how wild," she said calmly. It took supreme effort to keep her voice smooth. Her side hurt, her head hurt, her whole body hurt, but she didn't want Anton to know it.

He scrambled backward, both hands in the air. "Whoa. Where'd you get that?"

"Out of a box of cereal. Now get the hell out of here. I never want to see your face again."

"Is that thing loaded?"

"Wanna find out?"

"I don't know why you're so pissed off. It's

not like we've never done it before. What difference would one more time make?"

"The difference is that this time I don't *want* to do it. Now go back to your Sugar Mama."

He got to his feet and began backing toward the ladder. "You were never anything special, anyway," he said. "Look at you. You look like a damn bag lady."

That was uncalled for.

He glanced around the room. "Living here in this place like some nutty hermit. Thinking you could paint. Let me clue you in. You can't paint, Claire. Nobody wants to buy your crappy little paintings of crappy little grasshoppers and frogs." He pointed to himself. "I've been there. I've seen what people like. I've seen what they want." He pointed around the room, from one picture to another. "And nobody wants shit like this hanging on their walls." He swung around on his black shiny boots. He took a step toward the ladder. On the way, he swept up one of her pictures that had been knocked down in the fracas. He grabbed the ladder, swinging himself onto the rungs, her picture mashed between his palm and the side rail. He climbed down partway, then stopped.

"You wanna know something else?" he said, his head sticking out of the opening. "*You* were never anything special, either. Just another lay. You thought we had good sex, but we didn't. I've had a lot better."

He nodded, his mouth curled in contempt. "A *lot* better."

He was almost to the front door when she grabbed his jacket and tossed it down the hole after him. "Take your fucking gigolo jacket!"

She heard his angry footfall, heard the soles of his sissy shoes as he made his way back to get his jacket. As a finale, he pulled down the ladder, dropping it on the living room floor.

She listened, finally hearing the sound of a car pulling away, finally hearing it fade into the distance.

That's when she began to shake. The gun slipped from her fingers, clattering to the floor. She put a trembling hand to her mouth.

He hadn't raped her, yet she'd been violated. Emotionally, physically. And worse, by attacking her art, he'd raped her soul.

Darkness fell.

He'd left the front door open. She could tell because the cold found its way upstairs, and she could hear Hallie's toenails clicking around on the wooden floor. Kind of tap-dancing across the floor, the chunks of snow and ice that always clung to the pads of her feet making the sound even more distinct.

Claire knew she should climb through the opening in the floor. The drop wouldn't be bad if she lowered herself as far as she could before letting go. But she felt sick to her stomach. Instead of getting up, she crawled into the space between the couch and the wall. Once there, she cried.

Seventeen

It was stupid, going back. And dangerous. She'd probably called the cops. They probably had her place staked out. That was it. The thing on the news about his being presumed dead was a trick to flush him out. And he'd fallen for it. He'd been sucked right into their trap.

A novice would have known better.

But Claire. He couldn't get her out of his head.

Dylan had been waiting years for the opportunity to vanish, and here he was, risking everything to see Claire one last time before he rode off into the sunset. It was nuts. So he'd told himself he'd just swing by her place on the way to wherever the hell he was going, pay for the repairs on her Jeep, plus return the money and backpack.

He bought a car from a guy for a grand. Front-wheel drive. Two hundred thousand miles on it. What more could he ask for? He'd also picked up some necessities, like basic clothing and a new jacket.

It was dark when he turned down the snow-packed lane that led to her house. He'd planned it that way. Darkness seemed the way to go, in case somebody was watching her house.

He pulled up next to her Jeep, deliberately avoiding the motion light's target area.

The front door was standing wide open. There were no lights on inside.

A trick? A trap?

He shut off the engine, grabbed the backpack, and slowly got out of the car, his heart pounding a warning. He moved toward the door. The motion light came on, almost blinding him. A second later, Hallie nailed him, hitting him hard in the stomach with both front paws. He rubbed her good behind the ears, all the while keeping his eyes on his surroundings. Hallie dropped back to the ground and circled him, making a whining sound Dylan didn't like at all.

Remaining outside, he reached around the corner and turned on the living room light. He waited a moment, then slowly looked inside. Hallie had been going in and out as she pleased. There were wet spots where she'd tracked in snow.

He told himself to run, to get the hell out of there. Any moment, he was going to be surrounded by a bunch of weekend warriors in flack jackets, pointing sniper rifles between his eyes.

He spotted something on the floor. A piece of

paper. Torn. Dirty. Familiar. He stepped inside and picked it up.

Even though it was torn and smudged and wet, he still recognized it. Claire's picture. The one of the grasshopper, the one he'd liked so much.

The backpack slipped from his numb fingers. "Claire!"

He ran to the bedroom and turned on the light. Nobody. Nothing disturbed. The bathroom was the same way. In his haste, he'd missed the ladder the first time through. Now he spotted it lying near the wall, as if someone had angrily tossed it there.

He grabbed the ladder and positioned it through the hole in the ceiling. Not wasting time to test its stability, he shimmied up, climbing so fast that the top lifted away every time he grasped a new rung.

He jumped from the ladder and quickly found the light switch.

Everything hit him at once. The broken easels, the pictures—Claire's pictures—torn, rumpled, stepped on. This was no random act of violence. It was deliberate, calculated, executed out of hatred or spite.

His gaze fell to the gun.

Holy mother.

It was lying in the middle of the room, half covered by a notebook. He picked it up. He stared at it for a moment, holding it in both hands. He lifted his head, no longer seeing the room but looking into tomorrow, into infinity.

"Claire!"

*　　*　　*

Dylan.

Claire pressed a hand to her mouth. In the process, paper rustled. She'd forgotten that she was holding one of her torn pictures.

Her breath caught in her chest, tight as a spring, painful.

Footsteps moved slowly in her direction . . . until she saw a pair of workboots directly in front of her.

Not black shiny boots with pointy toes. These were real boots. Dylan's boots.

She wanted to wrap her arms around those boots and kiss them.

"Claire?"

She'd daydreamed about his coming back. She'd thought of him every day, every hour of the day. But she hadn't wanted him to see her like this.

"I . . . I, uh, was just back here looking for something. Just looking for something. Trying to find a pencil. I have this favorite pencil, you know. It's really good for shading in large areas. It has just the right tone to it. Not too dark, not too light. It's soft, too. So it doesn't press into the paper. I don't like it when a pencil actually makes a physical mark on the paper. When you draw, you aren't sculpting, you know. You're drawing. You don't want to carve up the paper. That's not what it's all about. Carving up the paper—"

"Claire, are you hurt?"

She lifted the picture closer to her face. With trembling fingers, she touched what she could see of the frog. "It's torn."

He crouched down in front of her. "Who did this?"

The barely controlled rage in his voice scared her. He sounded as if he wanted to kill somebody.

"It doesn't matter."

She was embarrassed to tell him that the person who'd trashed her studio, who had trashed her life, had been none other than her ex-boyfriend.

"It does matter."

She sniffled. "Don't be nice to me."

"Why shouldn't I be nice to you?"

"What makes you any different from him? You took my rent money. You wrecked my Jeep."

"I stopped by Jim's Garage and settled your bill there." He pulled something from his pocket. Money. "I'm here to pay the money I owe you, not destroy your work."

"Where'd you get that?" God, he's robbed a bank, she thought.

He tucked the bills in the pocket of her shirt. "It doesn't matter."

"It does matter!"

"Don't worry. I didn't rob a bank, if that's what you're thinking. You don't have that low an opinion of me, do you, Claire?"

She sidestepped that question. Instead, she brought up a couple of other reasons she had for distrusting him. "You tied me up and left me that way all night. You handcuffed me to my own bed. Now that I think about it, you're worse than he is." She wiped at her nose with the back of her hand. "I should hate you. I want to hate you."

He slipped the ruined picture from her and put it somewhere behind him. "Come out of there." Her grasped her by the forearms, exactly where Anton's hands had held her so cruelly. She let out a gasp and Dylan's hands sprang away.

"I can do it myself." Actually, she wanted to stay right where she was, only with her arms wrapped around his booted feet.

He scooted back while she crawled out from behind the couch. She shoved herself to her feet, dusted herself off, pushed back her hair from her face. "There," she said breathlessly. "Good as new."

Apparently Dylan didn't think so, because he let out a strange, choking, sobbing sound. "Jesus, Claire."

She looked down at herself. Her flannel shirt was torn. The top two buttons of her jeans were undone.

He reached for her. When his fingers made contact with the side of her face, she winced away.

"Who the hell did this?"

She shook her head, unable to speak.

"Why are you trying to protect the bastard?"

"I'm not."

He was doing something with her blouse. It took her a moment to realize he was unbuttoning it. He slid it from her shoulders, down her arms. "I'll kill him," he said under his breath.

That's what she was afraid of. It was bad enough that Dylan was wanted for fraud. He didn't need to add murder to his accomplishments. She looked down at herself, at the blue handprints Anton had left on her arms.

"It was that scurve Anton, wasn't it?"

"How did you know?"

"It had to be somebody who knew you. It had to be somebody who wanted to hurt you for a personal reason."

She tried to wrap her arms around herself, half to cover what her semitransparent bra was revealing, half because she was cold. "H-He didn't rape me."

Dylan slipped her shirt back over her shoulders, and buttoned what buttons were still there. Then he grabbed a blanket from the couch and wrapped it around her, pulling it tight in front. "Tell me the truth, Claire."

"He didn't rape me." Not physically, were the words she added to herself.

She found herself staring at him. Staring at him was better than thinking about what had just happened. Much, much better. She looked at him closely, to make sure he hadn't morphed into someone else the way Anton had.

He was still Dylan. But how had she forgotten that his hair was the color of Burnt Umber? And that his eyes were a cross between Davy's Gray and Emerald Green. If she were to paint his skin tone, she would have to use Golden Ochre lightened with Titanium White.

"What are you doing?" he asked. "Why are you looking at me like that?"

She brought up her hand and touched his face. "Painting you in my mind." She laughed at his puzzled expression. "I do that sometimes. Would you do something for me?" she asked, looking up at him, reaching for his hand.

"Anything."

He didn't ask what she wanted of him first. It was just, Anything.

"Would you hold me?"

He caught her fingers, then brought them to his mouth. His lips were incredibly soft and warm. He kissed her fingertips, then kept her fingers there. And she found herself wishing that her lips were there where her fingers were.

"I heard that they aren't looking for you anymore," she said quietly.

He lifted a strand of her hair. He brought it to his lips, kissing it. "They think I'm dead," he said in the same way someone else might say, They think I'm living in Peoria.

"You've probably served enough time for your crime, anyway."

"That's what I thought."

"And you've learned your lesson."

"Of course."

"You'll never take anything that isn't yours ever again."

"Oh, no."

Five minutes later, they were sitting on the couch with Claire's legs draped across Dylan's lap, his arms around her, her head resting on his shoulder.

She wished he would kiss her. But then he'd made it clear that he didn't think of her that way. "Can I ask you something?"

"Ask away."

"Do I really smell like mothballs?"

He laughed, pulling her closer. He pressed his face to her hair in what she took to be a brotherly gesture. He sniffed. "I don't know what you smell like. I can't place it."

She hoped it wasn't body odor. There were times when she was working on something and she'd completely lose track of time, when she would actually forget to take a shower and forget to eat. But she'd just showered and washed her hair that morning. Hadn't she?

"It's not mothballs. It's like . . . cedar or some other kind of wood. Now I have it. You smell like a blanket that's been stored in a cedar chest."

How lovely. She smelled like something old that had been kept in the dark too long.

Eighteen

Claire couldn't get warm.

She'd tried adding more wood to the fire. She'd tried a hot bath. But fifteen minutes later she was shaking all over again.

With Dylan in the kitchen banging pans around, she sneaked out the back door to the sauna. Teeth chattering, she turned on the thermostat, rotating it up to 200 degrees, thankful that the sauna was electric and would heat up fast.

She sat down and waited, all bundled up, her cap pulled down over her ears, her mittened hands tucked under her armpits. And while she waited, she thought about her artwork and the proposal Anton had destroyed.

Could she start over?

Did she want to?

The deep chill that had settled all the way to her heart began to dissipate, the heat of the sauna beginning to seep into her bones. The thermostat on the wall was moving up rapidly. It was already over a hundred.

She took off her coat and mittens, then stripped down to nothing, wrapped a bath towel around her, and sat back down, her head against the wooden wall, and closed her eyes.

She was drifting in and out of a wonderful stupor when the door flew open so hard it banged against the wall.

She sat up straight, her heart pounding.

Dylan stood in the opening, his coat unbuttoned, head bare, out of breath. "I didn't know what the hell had happened to you." He sounded angry and relieved at the same time. "Why didn't you tell me you were coming out here? I've been looking all over for you."

She shivered. "You're letting in cold air."

He closed the door, blinking his eyes against the semidarkness.

She leaned her head against the wall again, closing her eyes. "There's another towel there if you're modest."

She heard him shrug out of his coat, heard him kick off his boots.

"It's like a sauna in here," he joked in a voice that was still a little breathless. "I've always wanted to say that, but never had the opportunity."

"You've never been in a sauna before?"

"Nope."

"I love it. You can feel it all the way to your toes, all the way to your bones."

"I never could figure out why people would pay money to sit and sweat."

She opened her eyes just enough to peek through her eyelashes.

He was in the process of taking off his shirt. That was followed by his jeans, then a pair of white jockey shorts.

He was so tan. Where had he gotten so tan? The only place that hadn't been exposed to the sun was a strip of pale, firm, muscled bottom just slightly wider than his jockey shorts.

How had he gotten so gorgeous?

And why the hell wasn't he the least bit interested in her? She thought about the horrible things Anton had said about her. Was she really so unappealing? So unattractive? So lacking in sexuality? Maybe Anton was right. Flannel shirts and workboots probably didn't do a lot for a guy.

Dylan was reaching for the towel when she beat him to it, her eyes wide open, her arm stretched toward him, towel in hand.

It was hard to keep her gaze locked on his, to keep her eyes from drifting southward, but she managed. She also had excellent peripheral vision. And she thought she detected some signs of life down there.

Keeping his eyes on hers, he slipped the towel from her fingers. Then, with what seemed to her a studied hesitance, he wrapped it around his waist, low above his hips. Then he sat down, not right next to her but close. Close enough for her to touch him if she got the notion.

"Are you going to press charges?" he asked.

Anton. Why did he have to bring up Anton? She was trying to forget about him, at least for the moment.

She stood and poured some water on the hot coals. It sizzled, releasing a cloud of steam. When she turned around, Dylan was staring at her, and not at her eyes this time. He swallowed, his gaze tracking back up to her face.

The towel she'd wrapped around herself wasn't all that big. Rather skimpy as a matter of fact, just barely covering the important areas.

So. He wasn't as disinterested as he pretended to be.

"I don't know." Perspiration had gathered between her breasts to form a pool. The pool broke, sweat trailing to her navel. "Probably not."

She sat back down, retucking her towel, pushing the damp hair back from her face.

She heard him exhale. Heard him mutter something under his breath.

"What?"

"It's hot as hell in here."

"It's supposed to be."

"Since I know you're not lost or something, I'm gonna leave."

"You just got here."

"I changed my mind."

This time she didn't even try to pretend she wasn't watching.

He dropped his towel and reached for his jeans.

"How did you get so tan?" she asked, openly curious. Her gaze moved from his face, down his chest, then lower.

Oh, my. It was her turn to swallow.

He slipped first one leg into his jeans, then the other. He had a little trouble getting the rest of himself situated, wincing as he pulled up the zipper.

"The desert."

"The desert? Where?"

He shrugged into his flannel shirt. "Arizona."

"As in Phoenix?"

"As in the middle of nowhere." He stuffed his feet into his boots, but didn't tie them.

"And you ran around in your underwear there?"

"Cutoffs."

He was about to step out the door when she stopped him. "You forgot something." Dangling from one finger were his underwear. He grabbed them from her and stuck them into his coat pocket.

That night, as they sat in front of the fire—Claire curled up in her usual corner of the couch, her feet tucked under her, and Dylan on the floor, his back against the couch—Dylan made an offer Claire couldn't refuse.

"Why not let me take care of everything while you paint, while you put a new proposal together. You won't have to worry about the dog, or the wood, or groceries or anything. Just concentrate on your painting."

"And what do you get out of this? I can't afford to pay you anything."

"A place to stay. For a while."

"A place to hide, isn't that what you mean?"

"I need some breathing space. I need some time to think, to figure out what I should do. And what if Anton comes sniffing around here again? I'd sure as hell like to be here if that happens."

She wouldn't admit it, but she'd been rather worried about that herself.

"What do you say? I'll be Mr. Mom and you can concentrate on your proposal."

"I'm not sure I even want to put a proposal together now. I don't know if I can start all over."

"Come on, Claire. Don't chicken out on me."

"Maybe I'm just being realistic."

"You're good. Don't let a fear of rejection keep you from finding out just how good you are."

When he put it that way, what choice did she have?

Dylan turned out to be a halfway decent cook— something he'd learned in prison, Claire decided.

And he'd been perfectly serious about taking care of everything so she could paint. He repaired the broken easel. He chopped wood. He fed the dog. He got groceries. He cleaned the house. He did the laundry. He even cleaned out the bucket o' barf so he could remove the ashes from the woodstove.

It didn't take her long to realize that he didn't go about chores the way most people did. He was either the laziest man alive, or the most ingenious.

He didn't haul the wood he chopped. Instead, he got it to the front porch by way of a conveyor belt he'd put together with an old motor and treadless tires, cut into long strips. He didn't just feed the dog. He made a kind of Mouse Trap Game contraption, that, when you pushed a lever, dumped dry dog food from a coffee can to slide down a trough to finally end up in Hallie's dish. Most of the time. If it snowed, his invention didn't work. That bothered him.

"I need to come up with a way to keep the snow off the trough. Maybe heat tape attached to the bottom so the snow will melt when it hits it."

Housecleaning for him was a game. He somehow had it figured so he could dust and sweep the entire house in eight minutes and thirty seconds.

And then there were the dishes. She kept wondering how he got them washed, dried, and put away so fast until one evening she caught him spraying off a plate, then stacking it in the cupboard without drying it.

"You've been washing dishes without soap?" she asked in disbelief.

He shrugged, hosed down another plate, and stuck it in the cupboard.

"What the hell's this?"

Claire looked up from the worktable to see Dylan standing on the ladder, visible from the waist up. Dangling from one finger was a pair of her panties.

"Underpants." It was rather erotic to see him holding something of hers that was so personal.

"You actually *wear* this?"

He, on the other hand, was acting as if the scrap of fabric didn't do anything for him. "What's the purpose?" He held it open with his two index fingers, the elastic stretched tight. It was just a little triangle of nylon attached to a couple of pieces of elastic.

"It's called a thong."

"Why?"

"I'm not sure. Maybe because of the way the elastic fits . . ."

"No, I mean why do you wear this kind of thing?"

She put down her paintbrush. "I guess it's my one concession to femininity."

He balled it up and stuck it in his shirt pocket, shaking his head.

"Don't you think it's sexy?"

"Sure, but Claire, you don't need to go around wearing some torture device to be sexy."

It was the first time he'd ever said anything that made her think he might find her attractive.

"Actually . . ." She gave him a little smile. "They aren't uncomfortable at all. They're rather liberating. Almost like having nothing on at all."

"Is that right?" He was staring at her in a contemplative way.

She picked up her brush. "That's right."

With Dylan's help, Claire got her proposal finished. It wasn't as complete as the first one would have been, but it was there—enough, she hoped, to give the card company a solid idea of her capabilities, limited though they might be.

She packaged it up, then drove to Fallon and mailed it to her agent. As soon as it was no longer in her hands, she felt drained, wiped out. Before going home, she stopped at the gas station. When she was inside paying, she spotted a gossip magazine near the counter. And right there on the front was a picture of Anton. It seemed he was now living on the Riviera with the rich widow.

Should she tell Dylan? Her proposal was done. Anton was out of the country. There was no reason for Dylan to stay. But if she said something to him, then he would think she wanted him to leave. And she didn't want to him leave.

One of these days she'd tell him.

The next day she noticed something she may have been too busy to pick up on before. There was a studied aloofness about Dylan. Whenever they were in the same room, he would take off, seeming to have something of the utmost importance to do.

"You're not my slave," she told him one evening when he wouldn't take the time to sit down and eat. "That's not what any of this was about."

"I ate earlier. When you were in town."

"It would have been nice if we could have eaten together."

"I didn't think about it. Food to me is just fuel."

She didn't believe him.

Why was he avoiding her?

She took a good long look at herself. At that very moment, she was wearing a pair of bib overalls that were incredibly soft and comfortable. They were also faded and torn and paint-splattered. Her hair—she couldn't remember when she'd last really even thought about it. And makeup? Had she worn any lately? Come to think of it, she'd have to wonder about any man who *did* find her attractive.

The next morning Claire stood at the window, watching Dylan chop wood. Even though it was cold out, he'd stripped down to a T-shirt. And when he stopped to wipe the sweat from his forehead, steam rose from his hot body.

She couldn't spend her days mooning over

somebody who had no interest in her. You couldn't make someone feel attracted to you.

At least that's what she told herself . . . until she came across the voodoo doll. She was going through the desk, looking for stamps, when she found it. Until that moment, she'd completely forgotten about the doll. The little pin was still in its chest—proof that it didn't work. Dylan hadn't fallen head over heels in love with her. And would she have wanted him to anyway? No, of course not. Another complicated relationship was the last thing she needed, especially one with somebody who was wanted by the police. She'd let him stay at her place in hopes of helping him find some direction, giving him a chance to get himself together, figure out what he was going to do.

All the same, she couldn't quit staring at the voodoo doll. Maybe she'd been going about this all wrong.

She searched through the drawer until she found another white pin. This time, instead of sticking it in the heart, she poked it in the crotch.

The front door opened, cold air blasting in, along with Dylan and an armload of wood.

Claire stared, the doll in her hand.

His face hidden by the wood, Dylan kicked off his boots and strode across the room, moving in the direction of the stove.

Galvanized into motion, Claire hurriedly stuffed the voodoo doll into the desk and slammed the drawer.

Nineteen

Over two weeks had passed since Claire mailed her material to New York, and in that time neither Dylan nor Claire had mentioned Dylan's pending departure. The possible return of Anton was the only reason Dylan had to give for delaying a journey into new and uncharted territory, if the question were to come up. That was until the day he went to town to get groceries and spotted the tabloid while waiting in the checkout lane. He picked it up. Was it Claire's Anton? The story fit. The guy was an artist having an affair with a rich widow. If it was Anton, then Dylan had no excuse to linger.

He slipped the tabloid back into its slot, hoping that Claire wouldn't see it.

It had been nice, he told himself as he drove back to Claire's, living a reclusive life in a mountain cabin with a beautiful woman, making love to her day and night, if only in his dreams. And that's what it had been. A dream. A fantasy. She was probably expecting him to leave, waiting for him to leave, but was just too nice to ask when that leave-taking would happen. She'd been acting weird around him lately and now he finally figured out why. What did they say about houseguests? They were like fish: After three days they started to smell. He should be pretty ripe by now. At least when he left, he wouldn't have to worry about that sleaze, Anton, bothering Claire.

When he got to Claire's, she met him at the door, screaming.

His heart slammed against his chest. At first, he just naturally thought something bad had happened. But then he realized she was happy. She was jumping up and down, screaming and laughing, and trying to talk. She kept waving an envelope in front of his face.

"They liked it!" she shrieked.

He laughed along with her, still not having a clue.

"My proposal! Cardcity liked my proposal!"

The pictures. The proposal for the card line. That was fast.

"This is a letter from my agent!" She grabbed him by both arms and continued to jump up and down. "They've made an offer!"

One minute she was smiling and laughing at him. The next, she was pulling his head down, kissing him.

Oh Lord.

Sweet, sweet Lord.

It wasn't a long kiss. Or a short kiss. Or a sisterly kiss. Or a sexy kiss. It was just a kiss.

And it knocked him out. Sent his head spinning.

She let go of him and jumped away, running around the room, waving the letter in the air. She jumped on top of the couch, the cushions popping up around her feet.

And all he could think about was the kiss. All he could think about was how bad he wanted her.

Set the twilight reeling. Now he understood what Lou Reed meant.

She jumped off the couch. "John—my agent—says not to take their first offer. But I don't know." She stopped in front of him, arms at her side, her chest rising and falling. Her eyes shined. *She* shined.

She couldn't stand still. She rushed past him, and when she did, he caught a whiff of the cedar scent that permeated her hair. He could still feel the sweet soft imprint of her lips against his.

She stopped in front of him again, this time with her legs apart, hands on hips. "What do you think?"

"Think?" *I think I love you.* Son of a bitch. Partridge Family lyrics were popping into his head. He should have stuck with Lou Reed.

She may have been wearing a pair of faded bib overalls and a waffle-weave shirt, but Dylan knew that underneath all that was a lacy, transparent bra that cupped her lush breasts, plus a tiny wisp of fabric between a pair of soft, inviting thighs.

"About the offer? Should I accept now? Or hold out? I'm afraid if I hold out, they might change their minds. I don't want them to think I'm difficult to deal with."

I think I want you.

I think I have to have you.

Somewhere between her kiss and bedtime, he put the groceries away. Sometime in there, they ate something. Sometime in there, he took a shower, and she took a shower, and they both went to bed, Claire in her room, Dylan on the couch.

But he couldn't sleep. No way in hell could he sleep.

He kept thinking about her, wearing those little bitty strings she called panties. And those lacy, see-through tops she called bras.

But then, somewhere about midnight, he must have dozed off, because he came awake all hot and horny. He tossed back the covers and swung his feet to the floor. Normally the floor would have felt cold under him, but he was burning up. He peeled off his damp T-shirt, leaving him wearing nothing but a pair of flannel boxer shorts. Then, barefoot, he made his way through the dark to the kitchen, opened the refrigerator, and pulled out the container of water.

He stood there in the open door, drinking from the water bottle, the cool blast from the refrigerator hitting him full in the bare chest. He put the bottle back on the shelf. Instead of closing the door, he leaned his head against one arm, closed his eyes, and just stood there.

"Having trouble sleeping, too?"

He straightened to see Claire standing there, bundled up in her heavy coat, that goofy hat, a pair of clunky boots, and bare legs.

"Claire," was all he could think of to say.

"I couldn't sleep so I decided to start the sauna. It should be hot by now. Want to join me?"

He continued to stare.

"I've got magazines." She held up an issue of *Rolling Stone*. "I've got food." She held up a box of crackers. "You're not supposed to eat in a sauna, but I didn't think crackers would hurt. And I've got something to drink." She held up a bottle of wine.

He was sure one of those came with every sauna installation.

He slammed the refrigerator door, leaving them in total darkness. "I don't know." He rubbed his still perspiring forehead.

"I'll get you a towel." She shoved everything she was carrying into his hands.

He heard her clunking away toward the bathroom, saw the light come on, then go off.

Then she was back. "I came through here earlier, and you must have been dreaming. You were moaning and thrashing around. I almost woke you up to see if you were okay."

A dream? Oh, yeah. Now he remembered. Oh, wow. No wonder he'd come awake with the covers twisted around him. No wonder he'd come awake with a hard-on that hurt all the way to his brain.

Apparently her eyes had adjusted to the dark because she was moving through the room like a cat. When she reached the back door, she stopped and he ran into her. "Aren't you going to get a coat?"

"No. It's not far."

She laughed, still wound up from the afternoon's news. "You have to at least get something on your feet."

He wiggled his toes, realizing he was wearing nothing but the boxers. She was probably right. He handed all of the paraphernalia to her. Then he went all the way back through the house to the front door, running into the wall twice, bumping into Hallie, who just groaned her dog groan, before returning to where Claire waited at the door. He dropped his boots to the floor and stuck his feet inside, not bothering to tie the laces.

"Lookie here," he muttered in his best country accent. "I've done gone hillbilly."

She laughed and flicked on the deck light. They stepped outside into the chill night, their breath coming out a vapor in front of their faces. "We could get really hot, then run outside naked and roll around in the snow like they do in Alaska or someplace cold," Claire said, hurrying to the building that housed the sauna.

He might just need to roll around in the snow. It would be better than a cold shower. "Sweden. I think they do that in Sweden. And Finland. And Russia." He didn't think he needed to remind her that this *was* someplace cold.

Inside the sauna, with Dylan standing a foot behind her, Claire dropped her coat and kicked off her boots until she stood standing in front of him wearing nothing but one of her little string panty things, a bra, and her goofy hat.

He had this quick, snapshot image before she picked up a towel, wrapped it around herself, then grabbed everything he was holding and took a seat on the opposite side of the room.

"Are you going to sit down?" She frowned, looking suddenly concerned. "Are you feeling okay? If you aren't, a sauna wouldn't be good for you."

"I'm okay." He stepped out of his boots and crossed to sit down, leaving a good couple of feet between them.

"I've had this wine around for a long time. My grandmother used to make homemade wine. Did I ever tell you that?"

She was still buzzing, still running on pure adrenaline, while he was stunned, stupefied.

From somewhere, maybe it had been folded inside a towel, she pulled out a bottle opener and began fumbling around, trying to screw it in the cork.

"Here." He took it from her, screwed it in, then popped the cork from the bottle. "Are you sure we're supposed to be doing this? I don't know anything about saunas, but drinking alcohol in one doesn't seem like a good idea."

"We won't stay long. Oh, I forgot glasses. I can't believe I forgot glasses."

"That's okay. Here— You first." He handed the bottle to her. She took a drink, then passed it back. He took a drink. And then another.

"Elderberry wine," Claire said, taking the bottle from him and lifting it back to her lips. "Grandma made elderberry wine, dandelion wine, and blueberry wine."

They continued to pass it back and forth.

Before they knew it, the bottle was empty, and Dylan was sweating buckets.

"Did I ever tell you I don't usually drink? Oh, I tried to drown my sorrows when Anton left, but I just ended up hugging the toilet bowel. They say there's nothing worse than a champagne hangover, but a beer hangover's pretty damn bad, let me tell you.

"You have to watch out for this homebrew," she continued. "It sneaks up on you. It has a higher alcohol content than the stuff you get at the store."

"I hate to spoil your party," Dylan said, "but I'm going to have to get out of here."

"Too hot?"

"Yeah."

She was quiet a moment, long enough for Dylan to wonder what she was cooking up. It didn't take him long to find out.

"Let's go roll around in the snow, then we can come back inside."

He didn't answer.

"Come on. It'll be fun." She was already on her feet, dropping her towel to the floor. She grabbed his hand, pulling him up after her.

What else could he do but follow her out into the night, into the cold, cold night?

Steam rose from their hot bodies as soon as they stepped outside. With Claire still holding his hand, they ran through the snow, then threw themselves into a deep bank.

It felt good. After the smothering, feverish heat of the sauna, it felt *so damn good*. Kind of the way Dylan had always imagined snow would feel. Like a cool embrace on a hot day.

The light from the back door was enough for Dylan to see Claire lying beside him, acting like she was swimming the backstroke. He picked up a handful of snow and threw it at her, hitting her full in the face.

She screamed, picked up a handful of snow herself, and attacked, diving on top of him, rubbing the snow in his face, laughing the entire time. He grabbed her by both arms and rolled with her, over and over, stopping with her beneath him, her face half-covered with snow, her goofy hat lying a few feet away. He reached up and grabbed her hat, sticking it back on top of her wet hair so it was perched there, lopsided, kind of leaning over one eye.

"I don't want you to catch cold," he said, smiling down at her.

She laughed.

She had a laugh that sent him into a tilt, that sent little darts of electricity through his veins, all the way to his heart.

"You are unbelievable." How was it that he had found her? And why now, when his life had become so fallow?

He leaned down and licked some snow off her face, sliding his tongue over her cheek. Her laughter quickly faded. Her smiling mouth changed to that of open surprise. He bent his head again, and closed his mouth, first over her top lip, then the bottom, gently sucking off the snow and wetness.

There was a lingering sweetness there, a hint of the taste that he'd find if he were to go deeper into her.

"W-What are you doing?" she asked.

"Tasting you."

"I didn't think you thought of me like that."

"I changed my mind."

Her eyes, with their snow-kissed wetness, widened. "You have?"

He kissed the wet tip of her nose. It was cold. A tremor ran through her.

"Let's go back in the sauna," he said, moving off her, putting out a hand to help her up.

This time, when they stepped inside, the sauna felt as good to Dylan as the cold had felt just minutes ago.

Claire poured water over the hot coals. It sizzled. Steam rose. She picked up the towel she'd dropped earlier, wrapping it around her shoulders. Her earlier boldness had left her. Dylan realized that she suddenly felt shy, maybe self-conscious.

"Do you want to know what I was dreaming about earlier? When you walked through the living room?"

"Yes. Tell me. I love to hear about dreams."

"You."

"Me?" She asked it in a tone that held a sort of hopeful disbelief.

"We were doing things."

She had been staring at the vicinity of his chest. Now she looked up. She swallowed. "Oh?" It was a soft whisper. An inquisitive whisper. "What kind of things?"

"Are you sure you want to know?"

"I was hoping that maybe instead of telling me, you could . . . you know . . ." She made an airy gesture with one hand. Then she smiled up at him with some of her earlier bravado. "Show me?"

"Let's see." He looked toward the wooden

ceiling. "If I remember right, I was sitting down. And you—" As he backed up he took her by the waist, pulling her with him. He sat down on the bench. "You were facing me." He pulled her closer.

"Like this?"

She straddled his thighs with her legs and sat down.

He cupped the sweet curves of her bottom, left exposed by her tiny panties, and pulled her closer. "Of course we were both naked."

"Oh. Yes."

She put her hands to his shoulders. Her towel slid away. Her breasts were mounded above the softness of her low-cut bra, her nipples peeking out above the fabric like pink velvet.

"Wait. In my dream, you weren't wearing this silly-ass hat."

He pulled it from her head and dropped it beside them on the bench. Then he bent his head and placed his mouth first over one soft nipple, then the other. Her hands left his shoulders to dig her fingers into his hair. She began to move against him ever so slightly. He lifted his head and reached behind her to unhook her bra, sliding it down her arms, and dropping it somewhere beside them, all the while watching her as she looked back at him with dark, heavy-lidded eyes.

"In my dream, I was inside you."

He slipped his fingers beneath the elastic of

her panties, quickly finding her hot wetness. He stroked her, watching her head go back, watching her eyes close. "We were sweating, just the way we are now." He watched a trail of sweat trickle between her breasts. He bent his head and licked it, savoring the saltiness of her soft skin. He continued to stroke her. "And you were tight. And you were so hot. We were both on fire, both burning up."

She began making little keening sounds, sounds that told him she was winding up.

"Please, Dylan. Do something. Do it now."

She reached between them, quickly finding him through the slit in his boxer shorts, making a soft sound of appreciation as she freed him.

He had a sudden intrusive thought. "Claire, are you drunk?"

His question brought about a groggy reply, pulling her back from whatever kind of heaven people went to under such circumstances. "Drunk?"

"As in too drunk to make this kind of decision?"

"No. Absolutely not." She sounded close to panic. "Don't you dare change your mind on me. Don't you dare start trying to think for me. Or second-guess me."

"That's all I wanted to know."

With that, he lifted her onto him, sliding deep into her sweetness, at first just savoring the feel of her around him, at first just savoring *her*, savoring Claire. "Oh, Claire. You feel so good. So damn good."

He felt her hand on his cheek, lifting his face to hers. "Now will you kiss me?"

And he realized he'd never kissed her. Not a real kiss.

He moved his mouth over hers, sucking, kissing one part of her mouth at a time. He slipped his tongue deep inside, feeling the rough edge of her teeth, tasting the sweetness of the wine. She moaned. And then she pulled away to grasp the back of the wooden bench. She moved over him, using her knees as a lever to deepen the penetration.

She took him on a wild ride. It was like being on a roller coaster, and the car you were in was moving steadily up, higher and higher, and you knew it was just beginning, you knew things were going to change. And then suddenly there was the darkness, pitch black. And you went hurtling down so fast that there was no time to think about what was happening, all you could do was hang on.

He finally came back down, awareness slowly creeping in.

Claire was draped over him, her body limp and spent, her hair wet and sticking to his neck. They were both drenched in perspiration.

"Claire." Was she asleep?

"Claire."

She mumbled something against his neck,

and rolled her head around a little. "We've got to get out of here."

"I can't move," she muttered, one arm dropping beside her.

She was drunk. Drunk on her ass. For chrissake, what had he let happen?

"Claire. Come on."

He managed to wake her enough to lift her away from him and sit her on the bench where she immediately fell back to sleep, kind of collapsing head first onto the bench, her feet still on the floor.

He stood in front of her, grabbed her by both arms, and pulled her to her feet. Once she was upright, he draped both of her arms over his shoulders, and proceeded to walk backward toward the door.

At first, her feet just stayed where they were.

"Claire. Come on. Walk. One foot in front of the other. That's the ticket. There you go. Now we're going out the door. You're going to have to step up. Then step down. Thatta girl. There you go."

Cold air hit his back. He pulled it into his lungs, his sluggish brain immediately feeling clearer.

Son of a bitch. She was going to be pissed at him. Come morning, she was going to hate him.

He wanted to drop down in the snow, but while Claire was still upright and semiconscious, he thought he'd better just get her to the house, get her to bed.

The frigid air seemed to have a slightly reviving effect on her. Suddenly she stood up a little straighter. She looked toward the house, kind of squinting her eyes. "That my house?"

"Yeah. That's your house."

"Looks funny. Kind of swirly."

She was going to hate him. "That's because you're kind of swirly."

"I am?" She laughed.

Suddenly she put a hand to her chest. "Am I naked?" she asked, in shocked surprise, her spine straightening once more.

"Almost."

How in the hell had she gone from just feeling a little good, to drunk on her ass? One minute she'd just seemed like somebody who'd had a couple of drinks.

"Why'm I naked? More to the point, why'm I naked outside?"

"I'm trying to take care of that outside problem right now." This was a nightmare. Or some frat house dream.

She wagged a finger at him. "I know what you want. You want to"—she leaned close, then whispered very loudly—"have sex with me."

She took a staggering step. He caught her. "Come on, Claire."

Somehow he managed to get her into the house, kicking the door closed behind him. He half carried, half dragged her to the bedroom, dropping her across the bed. Her eyes were closed.

He shifted her around so her head was on the pillow, and her feet were where they should be. Then he pulled the quilts out from under her legs and covered her up.

"The bed's spinning," she said, throwing one leg out from under the covers and planting a foot on the floor. "If I put my foot on the floor, maybe it will stop spinning." She put an arm across her face. "Turn off the light. The light is hurting my eyes."

He turned off the light, then stood near the doorway, wondering what to do. He had his answer fairly quickly.

"Sick. Gonna be sick."

She threw back the covers, both of her feet hitting the floor at the same time. Her radar was excellent. She charged directly for the bathroom, never hesitating, never once staggering or taking the wrong turn. He followed the all-too-familiar sounds. He flicked on the light to see Claire, kneeling in front of the toilet, both hands on the rim, wet hair hanging on both sides of her face, naked except for a pair of thong underwear.

And he thought, this must be love. There she was. He'd probably never see her in a more humiliating situation, and yet he wasn't repulsed. And he wasn't disgusted. Instead he felt, well, he didn't think that honored was exactly the word for it, but it was as close as he could get. And he felt this kind of sweet affection that took him totally by surprise.

He grabbed her housecoat off the hook on the bathroom door and put it over her shoulders. Then he threaded her arms through it, one at a time. He smoothed the damp hair back from her forehead. "Done?"

She nodded.

"Want a drink of water?"

She shook her head.

"Want to get back in bed?"

She nodded.

He helped her up, then led her to the bed where he tucked her in all over again, noting the paleness of her skin, the purple smudges under her closed eyes, the way her lashes made a shadow on her cheeks.

I think I'm in love.

She's gonna kill me in the morning.

Twenty

☽

Claire moaned and rolled over in bed, hugging the pillow tighter. That didn't help. She moaned and rolled the other direction, wrapping the pillow around her swollen head.

Oh God. She felt horrible. *Horrible.*

Sunlight knifed its way through the window, shouting at her, screaming at her to get up. With her head feeling the size of a watermelon, she swung her legs to the side of the bed and slowly sat up. Bad idea. She lowered herself back down, missing the pillow completely to lie staring up at the ceiling. Her skin felt too tight for her body, her brain too big for her skull.

Thanks, Granny.

That had been some potent batch of elderberry wine.

What she needed was a shower. A shower helped everything.

She sat up again, pulling impatiently at the bathrobe that was twisted around her middle.

Carefully, she got to her feet, then moved very, very slowly in the direction of the bathroom, noting through a blur of agony that the house was quiet, that there was no sign of Dylan. Good. She didn't want him seeing her in this shape, didn't want him laughing in her face, telling her she should know better than to let herself get so stinking drunk that she ended up with the mother of all hangovers.

Poison. That's what alcohol was. Poison. She was just damn lucky she hadn't died.

The shower wasn't really a shower. It was actually a claw-foot tub that had been converted into a shower by hanging two white curtains on a curved rod. Claire separated the curtains and sat on the cold edge of the tub while adjusting the water temperature. She turned on the shower-head, stepped into the tub, and closed the curtain.

And she stood there.

And stood there, her eyes closed, her head tilted back, water soaking her hair, creeping in between each strand to sizzle when it hit her scalp.

Wonder how many brain cells I lost last night. Hundreds. No, that wasn't nearly enough. Millions. A million, billion, trillion.

The shower wasn't helping. She still felt like she'd been hit by a train. She couldn't remain upright another second.

She turned around, grabbed the edges of the

tub, and sat down, resting her shoulders against the curved back of the tub. The porcelain was cold against her skin. Under normal conditions, such a chill would have shot her back to her feet. Today it felt good.

She lay there with her eyes closed, the water from the shower hitting her full in the face, full in a forehead that had to have steam rising from it.

That was fun only for a little while.

Using her big toe, she turned off the showerhead, slid the metal drain lever to the right, leaned back, and waited for the tub to fill. While she waited, she found her green mesh scrubby thing, squirted some peach-smelling soap on it, then began to drag in across her body. She paused over her breast.

Was that a whisker burn?

No, couldn't be.

But she'd had a whisker burn before, and it certainly looked like a whisker burn. She gradually became aware of other sensations in other areas of her body, sensations that the agony of her hangover had completely overshadowed. Both of her nipples were a little sore. And between her thighs there was a tenderness, a sweet reminder of something she couldn't remember.

Oh Lord.

She thought back to last night, remembering Dylan in the sauna with her, drinking the elderberry wine. She even vaguely recalled running outside and rolling around in the snow. But after that . . .

Total blackout. Wasn't that what it was called? When alcoholics had hours of their lives they couldn't remember? But she wasn't an alcoholic.

Dylan. Where was Dylan? If they'd made love, the least he could have done was been around in the morning. She'd awakened by herself. Had he slept in her bed at all?

The tub was getting too full. She brought up her toe and shut off the water.

Why now? If they'd done it, why now?

The voodoo doll.

She put a hand to her mouth. *Oh, my God.* It couldn't be. And yet, the first time she'd stuck a pin in the doll's head Dylan had wrecked her Jeep and gotten a concussion.

She sat there until the water turned cold. Then, still moving with extreme care, she let the water out of the tub, dried off, put on her robe, and went to the kitchen to find some aspirin.

She had just swallowed two tablets when Dylan showed up.

"How are you feeling?"

She choked down a third chalky pill and turned around.

He stood with his hands in the front pockets of his jeans, one shoulder against the doorframe.

Her hand shook as she put down the glass on the counter. "Bad."

This was so awkward. He stayed where he was, keeping what seemed to her a wary distance. She pushed a lock of wet hair back from her face. If last night had been anything special to him, he wouldn't be hanging back like that. He'd come up to her, pull her into his arms, kiss her.

Once again she thought about the fact that he hadn't slept with her.

Had it been so awful?

Anton's words came back to haunt her. *You were never anything special. Just another lay.*

"Weren't you going to call your agent today?"

She'd completely forgotten about the contract with Cardcity. She put a hand to her head.

"When you're ready to go, I'll drive you to town. You don't look like you're in any shape to go by yourself."

"Thanks."

She had to get away, had to be by herself to sort things out. "I've got to go lie down for a while." She floated past him, not looking to the left or right, just intent on getting to her bedroom.

Did she even remember what had happened last night? Dylan wondered as he watched her disappear into the bedroom, closing the door behind her. She'd really been out of it. Or did she want to forget what had happened? It was entirely possible she was ashamed and embarrassed and wanted to forget the entire episode.

Easy for her.

It was all *he* could think about. He'd spent the rest of last night checking on her every few minutes, making sure she was okay. When morning came and she'd begun to stir, he'd disappeared, figuring it was a good time to chop wood. Lots of wood. But when he'd come back in to see her standing there in the kitchen, looking pale and small and confused, he'd wanted to go to her. He'd wanted to hold her, kiss her. Maybe even make love again, this time with her completely sober. He'd waited for some tiny sign, some infinitesimal hint that she remembered and that she didn't regret what had happened. But it had never come. And now he was going to have to spend the next several hours in close quarters with her. It was going to be tough.

Dylan insisted upon taking his car to Fallon, and Claire felt too horrible to argue. In fact, she felt too horrible to do much analyzing or putting of thoughts into words in order to fill the silence that followed them from her house to town.

The sun was too bright, reflecting off the snow, drilling a hole in her retina that went all the way to her brain. And his car was noisy, the way older cars were, and it smelled as if the previous owner had had a fondness for cigars.

"Here. Try these." Dylan took off his sunglasses and tried to hand them to her.

She shook her head. "No thanks."

"Go on. You need them more than I do."

She couldn't argue with that. She took them and slipped them on. Ahhh.

"Better?"

"Much."

Dylan turned into the 7-Eleven parking lot, pulling to a stop a few yards from the pay phone.

Claire stepped into the booth and closed the door, all the while aware of Dylan watching from his car. She dug out her phone card along with her agent's number and put the call through. It rang twice before she pushed the metal receiver down.

She couldn't go through with this. Who was she trying to kid? She was calling from a phone booth, for chrissake. She was a nobody from nowhere. She'd never finished college. She was a failure at everything. Sure, maybe they liked the pictures she'd sent them, but they were a fluke. Luck. She couldn't do it again. She couldn't keep up the quality. And even if she could, maybe the person who made the decision to buy was some goofball. Somebody who didn't know the market. Somebody who didn't know the difference between good and bad.

How awful to have her art shipped to every card store in the country, only to have people hate it, or worse yet, be indifferent. She was setting herself up for public ridicule.

She tried to visualize the sketches she'd sent them. In her mind she pictured a bunch of crude stick figures. There was the little stick froggie; the little stick turtle with his round head and dot eyes; the stick grasshopper.

Something was wrong. A terrible mistake had been made. A mistake she could fix. All she had to do was say one word: No.

The accordion door opened. Dylan squeezed himself inside, shutting the door behind him so they were smashed into the cramped glass booth.

"Something wrong?" he asked.

She hung up the receiver and continued to stare at it. "I can't do it."

"Here." He reached for the phone. "I'll dial for you."

She put a hand to his arm. "No, I mean"—this time she looked up at him through the dark sunglasses, giving added emphasis to her words—"I can't do it."

He stared at her, comprehension seeping into his features.

"I can't go through with it."

"Claire, don't do this to yourself."

She shook her head. "There's been some horrible mistake."

He picked up the receiver and tucked it under his chin. He dialed the phone card number. "What's the PIN?"

She told him.

Then he dialed her agent's number and waited.

"Claire Maxfield here to speak to John"—he lifted the paper—"Carpenter."

He handed the phone to Claire. "Tell him yes. That's all you have to do. Just tell him yes."

"John?" she said when she heard her agent's voice.

"Don't pass this up," Dylan whispered. "Don't do that to yourself."

Claire gripped the receiver with both hands, keeping her eyes on Dylan. "I've decided to accept Cardcity's offer."

John said something about not accepting so easily, something about letting them stew a little to see if they would come up with something better.

"No." She put trembling fingers to her sizzling forehead. "I want to accept their first offer."

"Are you sure?" From the tone of his voice, she could see he didn't think it was a good idea.

"I'm sure."

"Okay. You should see a contract in about a month. Oh, and Claire? Why don't you celebrate by getting yourself a telephone?"

She was thinking something along the lines of don't count your chickens before they hatch when she told him good-bye and hung up.

Dylan didn't move. She couldn't open the door, couldn't get out, until he moved.

"It'll be okay," he told her.

"For years I've been told that my work

stinks. How can the same stuff be bad one minute and good the next?"

"Maybe things aren't supposed to be easy. When things are too easy, we lose touch with what we feel passionate about. But when you have to fight for it, stand up for it, well, that would have to be a damn good feeling when you finally win. Where's the satisfaction in an easy win? Where's the *life* in an easy win?"

She understood what he was saying, yet his words didn't make her feel any more confident. Deep down she knew it wasn't just her art that was bothering her. For the moment it had taken a backseat to what had happened between her and Dylan.

She couldn't keep quiet any longer. "We made love last night, didn't we?" She hadn't intended for the tone of her words to hold such accusation.

He cupped her face in both of his hands, a tender gesture. "I'm sorry, Claire."

She pulled away from his touch. "I'm so *ashamed.*" Not that it had happened. Oh no. But the *way* it had happened. "I feel so *cheap.*"

"It was my fault." His voice was suddenly distant. Almost as if he were trying to sort something out in his head.

Someone honked.

Claire looked up through blurry eyes and dark lenses to see Libby frantically waving from her car, all smiles.

Claire attempted a feeble smile in return and a limp wave.

Oh, no. Libby was getting out of her car. She was coming over. She would be full of questions, full of curiosity.

"It's Libby," Claire said. "A friend of mine."

Dylan opened the door and inched his way out, with Claire following. In the glaring sunlight, Libby all smiles, Claire mechanically made introductions.

"Tell Libby your big news," Dylan said.

All the spirit had gone out of her, and he felt as if it was his fault. He wanted to see Claire's face light up the way it had last night when she'd gotten the letter.

He didn't know much about women. Nothing, really. There had been Olivia, of course, but that was different, and it had been years and years ago, another lifetime. There had been women in his life, but no relationships, nothing that had cracked the surface, nothing that had meant anything. He'd spent a lot of time simply existing, years spent in isolation.

He didn't want to go back there.

He noticed that Claire was still trying to figure out what he was talking about.

"My big news?" She put her fingertips to her lips, lips that were slightly swollen from kisses that he now understood had been too rough. Several times on the ride to town, he'd looked over to see her gently touching her mouth, a perplexed expression on her face.

"About your pictures," he said gently, coaxingly, part of his mind running on a totally different track, one he didn't want to be on.

He was going to have to leave. He'd known it before, but last night had made it a reality.

"You know the proposal I was telling you about?" Claire asked her friend. "I sold the idea to Cardcity."

Libby stared at her, the words finally sinking in. Her eyes got big. Her mouth dropped open. She shrieked in much the same way Claire had shrieked last night. Had that only been last night?

Libby grabbed Claire's hands and began jumping up and down. Then she grabbed a bewildered Claire and hugged her tight. "I'm so happy for you! I'm so happy!"

She pulled away, finally realizing that Claire wasn't sharing her enthusiasm. "What's wrong? Is something wrong? I thought this was good news."

Claire gave her a weak, watery smile. "I'm having cold feet."

"What you need to do is go home, take a nice hot bath, and then come over to my place for champagne. How does that sound?"

If possible, Claire turned even paler.

"Actually," Dylan told Libby, "Claire hasn't been feeling very well today. I think she's going to go home and go to bed."

Claire nodded. "I'm sorry, Libby."

Libby pulled down Claire's glasses and got a good look at her bloodshot eyes. "Oh, my. I see you've already been celebrating!" She slipped the glasses back into place.

Claire glanced over at Dylan, then gave Libby a feeble smile. "I guess you could say that."

Twenty-one

That evening, Dylan sat staring blankly at the TV, hopefully giving the impression that he was paying attention to what was occurring on the screen, when in fact he was basking in his own misery, telling himself how much Claire hated him, and how she had every right to hate him.

He suddenly realized he was watching a mindless sitcom. He pointed the remote at the TV, switching channels. National news. Did he really want to watch the news?

He was about to click again, when the lead-in got his attention. It was about his traveling companion of a few weeks ago.

"After living in seclusion for ten years, Daniel French came out of hiding and has again turned the chess world upside down. Since his return, he has been undefeated. He is now scheduled to play American champion Gregory Christianson. Does Daniel French still have what it takes? The world will be watching and waiting."

Dylan sat there, stunned. That son of a bitch. That sneaky son of a bitch. He clicked off the television, tossed down the remote control, then headed outside to chop more wood. At this rate, Claire would have enough fuel to last her the rest of her life.

The physical labor wasn't enough to keep Dylan's mind stagnant, to keep it from wandering, first to Claire, then to his childhood. . . .

There had been times at the orphanage when Dylan thought about running away. School was a bitch. He found he couldn't relate to Americans, even though he was one. How could he care about clothing styles and hairstyles, and cars and sports? At first his teachers decided he had a learning disability. Then a behavior disorder. Then they just plain kicked him out.

He was supposed to look for a job, but instead he started hanging around the strip where he discovered the mind-numbing combination of alcohol and dope. He never got into the heavy stuff. Maybe he would have if he hadn't met Uriah.

Uriah was an artist. He created chalk murals on the sidewalk, a boom box beside him, blasting out Leonard Cohen. It was weird, but he almost always drew pictures of people playing chess. All kinds of people of all nationalities. If he wasn't drawing people, then he was drawing chess pieces, beautiful, ornate masterpieces that should have been in a museum or something.

Uriah was obsessed with chess. He claimed it was an intellectual game that crossed all language barriers.

"Why the sidewalk?" Dylan asked the first time he saw him. "And why chalk? Why don't you do a mural out of paint, something that will last?"

Uriah leaned back on his heels and shoved a strand of blond hair out of his face. "Do you know what the word 'ephemeral' means, kid?"

Dylan shrugged, hands in the front pockets of his jeans, his back to the barred windows of a pawnshop. "Queer or something?"

The guy spelled it out in green chalk. "Go look it up and come back tomorrow and tell me why I like to put my pictures down in chalk."

"You're full of shit."

Dylan had been hanging around the street long enough to know how to beat a person at his own game.

Chalk Man didn't act like he even noticed.

That night, Dylan looked up the word. The next day he was back in front of the pawnshop.

The guy had his back to him, hunched over his picture, shading in a bright umbrella that loomed above the chessboard.

"It's something that doesn't last."

The guy never even turned around. He just kept dragging the chalk across the rough surface of the sidewalk.

"What's your own take on that?" the man finally asked.

Dylan had spent the last several months—hell, years—trying *not* to think. And here was a guy asking him to figure out why the hell he was drawing a beautiful picture on a sidewalk for people to walk on and spit on, and for the rain to finally wash away.

"It makes it something spiritual. Because real beauty is fleeting," Dylan said.

The arm with the chalk slowed.

Dylan continued. "On a large scale, it could be like life itself. If you think about how old the universe is and all, then life itself could be ephemeral."

The arm stopped altogether. Chalk Man turned around. And now Dylan could see he wasn't really much more than a kid. He didn't look like he could have been over twenty-five.

"Have you eaten lately?" he asked.

Uriah was just smart as hell. Maybe one of the smartest people Dylan had ever met. That's why it took Dylan by surprise to find out he was homeless.

Uriah knew everything there was to know about everything. He taught Dylan how to stack a deck of cards, he taught him how to panhandle effectively, he taught him how to survive on the street.

And he taught him how to play chess.

It was a game that Dylan's father used to play. When Dylan was four, his dad had held him on his lap at the kitchen table and shown him how the pieces were moved.

"He's too young for that," his mother had said, smiling.

"Never too young to learn to play chess."

Dylan had loved the horse—not the white horse, but the black one, the dark horse.

"It's a knight," his father had corrected.

"But it's a horse."

"Okay. Call it a horse if you want."

Uriah taught him strategies. Taught him how to use the pieces in combination to attack. Dylan could swear Uriah knew the name of every play ever made.

"I have a photographic memory," Uriah told him one day. "I don't forget anything. But some of the best chess players don't have the plays memorized. They play from the gut." He nodded his head. "But the good ones, the ones who make it big, they do both. You've got Moiseevich, who was a purely analytical player. And Adolf Anderssen, who was perhaps too emotional. And then there was Jacob Sax. His strength was the fake out, the con. If a player can be all three, then he's really got something."

"I used to be married," Uriah told Dylan one day. Uriah didn't usually talk about himself. "I had a house and a car. A decent job. Guess what kind of work I did?"

Dylan shook his head.

"Come on. Take a stab at it."

Dylan tried to picture his friend in some kind of employment, but it was impossible. "I don't know," he said, impatient, not wanting to play a guessing game. Why didn't the guy just tell him? "A plumber?"

Uriah slapped the back of his head. "Don't piss me off, kid." Most people would have gotten scared by that point, but Dylan egged him on. "I know." He pointed, acting surprised and honored. "You're that guy."

Uriah fell into his trap. "What guy?"

"You know. The guy."

"You want me to smack you again, li'l fucker?"

"The guy who sifts the cigarette butts from all the sand ashtrays in the world."

"You smart-ass."

He acted like he was going to smack him again, but instead, he got him in a headlock and gave him a Dutch rub. Except with Uriah, he didn't know his own strength. It felt like his knuckles were going to go right through Dylan's skull.

"So," Dylan asked him later. They were walking down the sidewalk, eating the sandwiches the cook at Barley's had given them through the back door. "What'd you used to do?"

Uriah seemed about to answer, when an old lady pushing a shopping cart appeared out of nowhere, almost bumping into him. Uriah jumped lithely to one side. The woman looked up at him and her mouth dropped open. She began babbling in Cajun, made the sign of the cross, and scurried away.

Dylan had picked up enough Cajun to know that she'd said something about Uriah having death on his face, or in his face.

"Man," Dylan said. "That was just plain freaky." He turned to look at his friend.

Uriah's face was ashen.

"Hey, you don't believe that crap, do you? The woman was some nutcase."

Uriah let out a nervous laugh. "Hey, if I die you can have all my stuff."

"That's bullshit. Come on. You were getting ready to tell me what you used to do."

Uriah handed his half-finished sandwich to Dylan. "I used to design arcade games."

Dylan laughed, thinking it was almost as funny as his ashtray joke. But then he realized Uriah wasn't kidding. His friend pulled out a pack of generic nonfilter cigarettes, offered Dylan one, then lit both cigarettes with one match. "I couldn't take the pressure," Uriah said, tossing the match to the ground and pocketing his cigarettes inside the black leather jacket he'd picked up at the Salvation Army. "There were always deadlines." He shook his head. "Too much pressure. I ended up in the nuthouse. I lost everything. My wife. My home. My car. But you know what's weird? I don't really miss it. None of it."

Dylan didn't believe him for a second. A family. A wife. He had to miss his old life. How weird to have lost it all. How did that kind of thing happen? The fact that Uriah had also lost his family made Dylan feel even closer to him, more like maybe *they* were family, brothers.

Two days later, Dylan couldn't find Uriah anywhere. He asked around. The first two people just shrugged. The third person told him Uriah was dead.

"You're lying," Dylan shouted, shoving the guy against a wall.

"No I'm not, man."

He put up his hand, in case Dylan decided to shove him again. "Some gang beat him up. Calling him a faggot. He's dead. He was put in a body bag and all. I'm not shittin' you, man. I swear, I'm not shittin' you."

Dylan turned and ran in the direction of the police station.

Everything was a blur. On the sidewalk, peoples' open-mouthed faces turned in his direction. He knocked a bag of groceries from a woman's hands, but continued running, finally reaching the police station, stopping at the first desk he came to.

"Yeah, we picked up a John Doe in the red light district," the officer said, his mouth full of food. How could he eat at a time like this? Didn't he have any respect for the dead? For the living?

"Where?"

The man pointed with his sandwich. "Four blocks down the street at the morgue."

It was Uriah.

He didn't look bad. Not really. Dylan was glad he didn't look bad.

Dylan turned and ran back into the street. He ran and ran, all the way to the wharf. He stared out across the gulf. Life was so hard. Life was so damn ugly. He wanted to jump in and keep swimming until he couldn't swim anymore.

The next day, he went to the spot where Uriah had slept. He hadn't used any of the shelters, preferring to have his own spot under a bridge not far from the ocean. There Dylan found Uriah's magic cards and Leonard Cohen tapes. He also found a notebook with page after page of chess moves and chess strategies, most of which Uriah had taught him.

And there was a chess set. Handcarved, a timeless replica of the fleeting, intricate, beautiful chess pieces Uriah had drawn in chalk.

Dylan slowly picked up the black knight, feeling its weight, its perfect balance.

So far he hadn't cried. But now he broke down and sobbed.

Dylan was sixteen.

After Uriah died, Dylan couldn't stay out of trouble. He was always getting thrown in jail for loitering, or breaking curfew, fighting, and underage drinking . . . until one of the cops noticed how much he liked chess and told him about a club in town for kids. He even offered to take Dylan to the meeting.

At first, Dylan felt so damn out of place he wanted to turn around and run. All the kids there were decked out in brand new clothes with their shiny faces and neatly parted hair. Rich kids from rich families. He didn't belong. He didn't want to belong.

But it only took him a short while to realize they had more things in common than he'd thought. There was the obsession with chess, yeah, but there was more. For years, Dylan had been picked on and made fun of because he was different. So had these kids.

Dylan had first been subjected to verbal ridicule from his uncle, then by the other kids at the orphanage. He didn't know how or why things were so wacko, but that's the way it was when you were smarter than your peers. They came at you like a pack of rabid dogs. He'd once read how horses would attack and sometimes kill a white horse in their own herd, because the white horse stood out from the rest. Apparently people hadn't evolved all that much. He was living in a place where being smart was a handicap, but fortunately he'd recognized that twisted fact at an early age. He'd learned to play dumb in order to get along with the rest of the herd.

With these kids, he could be himself. Or at least a version of himself.

He began competing, first on a local level, then state. And when he began competing, things moved fast. There was no holding him back. Maybe it was because chess was all he had, or maybe it was something for him to pour himself into, to vanish into, so he didn't have to think about anything. Whatever it was, Dylan became the equivalent of an overnight success. By the time he was nineteen, he'd become an international chess champion with a handful of high-stakes games behind him that had made him a millionaire. His picture was plastered on the cover of hundreds of magazines. The paparazzi gave him no peace. Even the legitimate press hounded him. Two years after becoming an international chess champion, Daniel Dylan French quietly disappeared.

Dylan was twenty-one.

Twenty-two

Claire pretended to be resting, pretended to be sleeping off her hangover. She heard the front door slam. She gave Dylan ten minutes, to make sure he wasn't coming back immediately, then she jumped out of bed and hurried to the living room, moving softly in her wool socks. She went straight to the antique desk and pulled out the voodoo doll. The pins were still there. One in the heart, one in the crotch. She pulled the pin out of the heart and stuck it in the crotch, along with the other pin. She lifted one of the doll's little white legs, reading the tiny print.

A libido gone stagnant?

The front door opened.

Claire shoved the doll back in the desk, quickly slamming the drawer. Then she waited to see if the new pin in the very important spot would have any effect.

Dylan kicked off his boots, then padded across the room in his gray wool socks, a load of wood in his arms. He put the wood down near the stove, then straightened. Claire sat there looking at him, trying to keep her expression neutral.

"What?" he asked.

"Nothing."

"You have a strange look on your face."

"You're leaving, aren't you?"

He kind of gave his head a little shake, her directness catching him off guard. "It's about time, wouldn't you say?"

"When?"

"First thing in the morning."

"Oh." So soon. Too soon.

Here she'd been waiting for him to throw himself on her, and he was planning his big getaway. How stupid of her. She didn't believe in voodoo dolls. And she'd never been the coy, flirty type, either. She couldn't saunter up to him, walk her fingers up his arm, hang on him, and giggle in his face. And she had the feeling he wouldn't like it if she did.

She had a stomach-churning thought. Maybe that's what she'd done last night.

"You still sick?" he asked. "Maybe you'd better go lie down."

She nodded and walked past him, humiliated that her close proximity had absolutely no effect on him.

That night Claire lay in bed, hoping against hope that he would come to her. That the voodoo doll would do its stuff. But he didn't come.

Stupid voodoo, she thought. What good is a voodoo doll if you can't put a spell on somebody? She kept thinking about things she could do to make him stay, but the only thing she came up with was handcuffing him to her bed again.

Up until that moment, Claire had forgotten about the handcuffs, which were still padlocked to the bed, hidden from sight, having slipped past the mattress to the floor.

She didn't think handcuffing him would make him like her. She's tried that once.

What would he do if she handcuffed herself to her bed? She rubbed her face. She was getting dumber all time.

"Claire?"

She lay there perfectly still. Had she heard something, or just imagined it?

"You awake?"

She scooted up in bed. "Yeah." She pushed her hair back from her face. Had the voodoo worked? "Can't you sleep?"

"No."

"Me either." That's a hint, Dylan.

He crossed the room, his feet a whisper against the bare floor. "I can't get you out of my head."

Yes!

"I don't know what's going on, but I can't quit thinking about last night. I've got to get out of here. Now. Tonight. I can't wait any longer."

Things had suddenly taken an unforeseen turn.

She scrambled to her knees, her mind racing. "You can't leave now, not in the middle of the night. How will you get gas? No gas stations are open now."

"I filled the tank yesterday."

"But you'll have to fill it again before morning. That car's a gas guzzler if I ever saw one. This is ridiculous. Childish. It's childish. Don't leave now. I'll worry." As if he cared, she thought. "I won't be able to sleep."

"I have to go."

He couldn't go. He couldn't leave, not like this. Plan A. What was Plan A? Oh, yeah. Oh, that was stupid. She couldn't handcuff him to the bed against his will.

Plan B, then. What was Plan B? Oh, yeah.

Fumbling in the darkness, she dug the handcuff key from the bottom of the drawer, opened the window next to the bed, then tossed the key as far and as hard as she could, and shut the window. Climbing back onto the bed, she reeled up the cuffs, looped them over the top railing, sat down on the pillow, and lifted her hands above her head, slipping her wrists through the metal bands. Then she clicked them shut, leaving herself dangling there in a totally helpless, sacrificial position.

There. Plan B. Handcuff *herself* to the bed.

"Claire?"

In the dark, she just had to imagine the baffled expression on his face.

"What *the hell* are you doing?" he asked.

Yeah, it baffled her, too. She was out of breath from all the running around, breathless from fear of his reaction. "You can't leave now. If you leave, I'll be handcuffed to this bed forever. Or at least until I die and they finally find my rotted carcass in the spring. I've thrown the key outside. I have no way of getting it."

"Why?"

"It's— It's a physical demonstration." She shrugged. "I like you."

"How much?"

He sounded very curious. Very curious indeed.

"A lot."

He laughed.

She sagged against the metal rails. Thank God he thought it was funny. Something so weird and kinky could have gone either way.

"Like a sister? Do you like me like a sister?"

"More like . . ." Her voice dropped to a husky whisper. "like a lover."

"Claire, if you wanted me to stay, why didn't you just say so?"

"Pride?"

"You're nuts. And I mean that in the nicest way."

"Thank you."

He laughed again. "I can't believe you threw the key out the window. It could take days to find it."

"This wouldn't be the time to start looking."

"Slightly off-kilter minds think alike."

He approached the bed. The mattress dipped until he was straddling her, a knee on either side of her hips. "You are such a surprise. A wonderful, wonderful surprise."

"That's one of the nicest things anybody's ever said to me."

He reached up and slid her pajama bottoms off her, dropping them on the floor beside the bed. Before removing the tiny scrap of fabric that barely covered anything, he admired her with his hands, sliding his fingers under the elastic band. Using both hands, he cupped her bottom, then followed the elastic *everywhere*. "How can this be comfortable?" he asked, his voice sounding a little tight.

"You get used to it."

"I'm glad about that."

She could already feel herself getting wet for him. The darkness made her brave, bold. With his help, she scooted her legs around so her knees were under her, so she was kneeling, her arms above and behind her head, her back arched, her breast aching for his touch.

He must have read her mind. With nimble fingers, he quickly unbuttoned her top, spreading the edges wide so that he could fill both hands with her breasts, the nipples pressed tautly against his palms. His hands, his big, wonderful hands, were everywhere. Rubbing her stomach, her thighs, between her legs. He cupped her bottom, his fingers delving between the two soft mounds of flesh. Starting at her navel, he licked her stomach, pausing to suckle her breast before continuing his journey to finally claim her lips. His tongue plunged deep into her mouth, hot and big, a promise of what was yet to come.

"Last night you took me on the wildest ride of my life," he whispered against her mouth. "But I think this is going to be even wilder."

Her mind was spinning away. But before things got completely out of hand, she had to tell him something.

"Dylan . . . ?"

His mouth was moving down her neck.

"In the drawer," she gasped.

"Mmm?"

"A key. There's another key."

He lifted his head. She sensed he was looking at her in the darkness. "Another key?"

"In the drawer."

"Later."

"Now. Get it now."

"Later. We'll find it later."

He began kissing her everywhere, licking her everywhere, until her entire body was aflame, until she completely forgot about the key, until she ached for his most intimate touch. He slowly tormented her, his hands freely roaming her body, the calluses sliding across her fevered skin.

"Bring your legs around my hips," he instructed. She wrapped her legs around him, her position on the bed, on the pillow, giving him the ripest access.

"Okay?" he asked.

She nodded.

"Claire?"

And she realized he couldn't see her. "Yes." She moved her hips—and felt the hot velvet tip of him against her swollen, feverish flesh.

"Yes," she repeated on an exhalation of air.

A hand supporting her lower spine, he entered her. He filled her.

She sensed that he was holding back, afraid of hurting her. And there was no way for her to pull him closer.

"Harder," she gasped, grabbing the rail above her head, lifting herself into him, showing him how she wanted him to be with her. She should have felt confined. Instead, she felt powerful, euphoric.

There was something about the position of their bodies or the elevated way he carried his erection that amplified the sensuality of his touch. Every stroke sent a hot, erotic wave through her, each wave more intense than the previous until she was setting the pace, increasing the speed of his passion with something close to madness until at last she shuddered. She tightened, contracting around him. He cried out, and held her tightly, impaling her with a thrust that lifted her from the bed.

Falling, falling . . .

Until they were limp, Dylan's damp hair against her thundering heart. "My God," he finally said, his voice a breathless, amazed gasp. He slid down her body so his head was resting on her abdomen. "My God."

She wanted to touch him, needed to touch him.

As if reading her mind, he said, "I've got to get the key, but I can't move."

"I want to touch you."

He moved over her to kiss her firmly on the mouth, and when he pulled away, she could feel his smile against her lips. He got to his feet and opened the drawer. She heard the sound of things being shoved around.

He turned on the light and continued his search.

"Claire?"

"Hurry."

"I can't find the key."

"Don't tease me."

"Claire, I can't find any key."

He pulled out the dresser drawer and dumped the contents on the bed. There wasn't much in it. Some pens. Scraps of paper. Matches. The orgasm book—they wouldn't be needing that. But no key.

Her fingers were getting numb. She wiggled them, trying to get the feeling back. "I know there is a key." Her voice rose in growing panic. "There has to be a key."

"I don't think calling a locksmith would exactly thrill you. It would thrill him, but not you."

She swung her leg in his direction. "I'm not in the mood for jokes."

"If I have to cut the cuffs off, I will," he assured her. "Do you have a hacksaw?"

"No."

"Tin snips?"

"No."

"Anything that will cut metal?"

"No!"

"Okay, okay. Let's not panic."

"I am panicking!"

He lifted the drawer, looking closely at where wood met wood. And there he found the small key wedged between the side and bottom of the drawer. He crawled across the bed. Then, kneeling beside her on the mattress, he stuck the key in the lock and turned it, freeing first one of her hands, then the other.

Claire watched as he brought a hand to his mouth, kissing her wrists one at a time. His eyes looked kind of sleepy, kind of like he was still turned on. She could relate.

Her gaze dropped to his arm, to the tattoo.

Forever Olivia.

She knew better than to mention her name, not now anyway. But soon. Soon she would ask him who Olivia was and what she'd meant to him. And what she still meant to him.

"That was probably one of my dumber ideas," she said, clenching and unclenching her fingers, trying to get the circulation back.

"Great ideas sometimes come with a few things to iron out. Nothing wrong with straddling that fine line between madness and genius."

She continued to stare at the strange symbol above the woman's name. She hadn't realized it before, but the tattoo looked old, as if he'd gotten it when he was a kid. It was a little out of focus, as if he'd grown after getting it. "Were you in a gang?" she asked.

When he saw the direction of her gaze, he looked down at his arm, then back at her. "More like a club."

From the abruptness of his tone, she could tell he didn't want to talk about it. It belonged to his past life, back with Olivia, back to a time he'd apparently rather forget.

He quickly put everything back in the drawer, then returned the drawer to the dresser, reached up, and clicked off the light. Then he slid into bed beside her and pulled her close.

Was he going to do what most guys did and fall instantly to sleep? She waited, listening to his even breathing. Was he asleep?

Ten minutes of waiting and wondering, she had to ask. "You liked the handcuff thing?"

"You were so quiet, I thought you were asleep," he said, sliding a hand down her hip, not sounding groggy in the least. "The handcuff thing? To say I liked it would be putting it mildly." There was a lengthy pause. "In fact, I don't think we'll ever be able to top it."

"I don't know about that." She rolled to her knees, pushed him firmly onto his back, and straddled him.

"But then again," he said in a tight, expectant voice, "you're so damn ingenious."

She wrapped her hand around him, feeling him harden. "I'm full of admiration for this particular part of your anatomy," she said.

"Yeah?"

"Not that the rest of you isn't nice, too, but this part . . ." She stroked him. She cupped him. "I'm just particularly taken with it." She leaned forward and kissed him, her nipples barely brushing the hair on his chest, sending little electrical impulses all the way to her belly.

She slipped down his body, her hands on his hips. She leaned close. Starting at the base of his shaft, she licked him with the tip of her tongue. Under her hands, his thighs tensed. She heard his indrawn breath. She followed a straight line all the way to the tip. She felt his fingers against her scalp, felt them digging into her hair.

He smelled and tasted like sweet, sweet love. She could never get enough of him, never get her fill. "I love how you taste."

"Claire," he groaned, his fingers digging into her scalp. "Sweet, sweet Claire. My God, woman. You're torturing me."

She slowly worked her way up his body, kissing his abdomen, his navel, his chest.

When she reached his lips, he was ravenous. He kissed her with madness, with the passion of ten men. "Down on me," he gasped, between kisses. "Come down on me." His hands were suddenly under her arms, pressing into the soft sides of her breasts. He lifted her onto him, filling her with his iron heat, amazing her anew at the power and breadth of him.

It had been her plan to be the one in charge, in control, but suddenly he turned everything around. He sat up and wrapped her legs around him. And then he twisted to the side, swinging his feet to the floor, and stood, his legs braced apart, holding her tightly to him.

"What are you doing?" she asked breathlessly.

"Bed's too soft."

With his legs braced apart, he lifted her, then dropped her against him, his body trembling, his muscles like rocks.

It was one of the most erotic things she'd ever experienced, each thrust taking her closer to the edge. He made love with such mindless abandon, such lack of self-consciousness. It was the most liberating, the most electrifying thing she'd ever known.

He finally reached a point where he couldn't stand any longer. Trembling, he dropped into a nearby chair, Claire wrapped around him.

The chair was like driving on a road with no shocks. He grasped her hips, lifting her in a rhythmic motion, his lips finding hers. "I don't know why we didn't do this before," he said, his breathing ragged. "We've got a lot of time to make up for."

"A lot of time," she agreed.

Her feet couldn't reach the floor. She had to move, needed to move, needed to participate.

"This isn't working," she finally said.

"I never claimed to be a grand master."

They went back to the bed, this time with Claire on the edge, Dylan standing.

Perfect.

"Now I know why they made these old beds so high."

"Claire?" he asked as he stroked her long and hard, his hips moving faster and faster.

"Mmm? You talkin' to me?"

"Tell me when you're having an orgasm."

"What?" Had she heard him right?

"An orgasm."

"Stop talking."

"I like to talk."

"You're distracting me."

"So? Tell me again how you like the way I taste. And the way I smell."

"You taste like love, like sex."

"Tell me everything you feel, everything you want."

"Touch me."

"What?"

"With your hand. Touch me."

"You mean like this?"

She threw back her head. "*Yes,*" came her faint whisper.

He knew just where to touch her, just what she wanted, just what to do to drive her wild. "Now," she gasped. "It's happening now."

"What?"

"An orgasm."

"I can feel it. I can feel you contracting around me, squeezing me."

"You're crazy. You're not supposed to analyze it."

"Crazy love. You feel so damn good. My God, woman. What have you done?"

"Done?"

"You've done something to me. Some kind of magic. Some kind of spell. Some kind of shit big spell."

Twenty-three

Several days later, Dylan was sound asleep when Claire pounced on the bed, waking him. She wore a heavy oatmeal-colored sweater and smelled of the cold outdoors, a smell he'd come to associate with her.

"Let's go do something," she said, her exuberance crashing into his groggy bafflement.

She was so damn wide awake. People weren't supposed to be so damn wide awake at—he twisted around to look at the clock—6:00 A.M. He groaned and let his head drop back down on the pillow.

She threw her leg across him, so she was straddling his hips. Then she slowly leaned forward, until her arms were crossed over his chest, her chin resting on her arms. "Come on." When she talked, her chin remained in one place while her head bobbed a little and her voice came out tight, like someone talking through her teeth. "I want to take you to some beautiful places."

He cupped her bottom with his hands, thinking about the sexy panties that were somewhere under a pair of faded jeans and long underwear. "You've already taken me to some beautiful places. In fact, I wouldn't mind going to some of those places again." He slipped a hand under her sweater. And then under something else that was thick and textured. And then under a tight tank top, to finally find her warm skin.

"I don't know," she said, smiling in a sexy, teasing way. "It took me about an hour to get all of this on. I thought we could drive up Highway 95 today."

"Why?"

"Because there's a frozen waterfall you just have to see."

"We can still do that," he said. "It's early."

She pushed herself to a sitting position, still straddling him. She crossed her arms in front of her, grabbed the hem of her sweater, and pulled it over her head. That was followed by an insulated cotton henley, leaving her in the tank top. She wasn't wearing a bra. He could see the sweet shape of her breasts beneath the soft, clinging cotton, see the hard outline of her nipples.

"I was just dreaming about you. And me," he told her, putting his hands behind his head so he could simply watch her.

"What were we doing?"

He smiled at her sleepily, still caught up in the hazy sensuality of the dream. "We weren't looking at frozen waterfalls."

She slid from the bed, unbuttoned and unzipped her jeans, and kicked them off. That left her in a pair of cream-colored, waffle-weave long-john bottoms and heavy wool socks. He didn't understand how such an outfit could be sexy, but it was. She slipped out of the long underwear, then the tank top, and finally the little strip of elastic.

"Seems a shame," he murmured, lifting the down comforter for her. "After all the work you went to getting all of that on."

"I know," she said, sliding in next to him, wrapping herself around his nakedness, her body hot in places, cold in others. "All that work."

Because he wasn't quite awake, their lovemaking took on a different tone. It wasn't the hot passion they'd shared in the middle of the night. This time it was slow, kind of sleepy, and oh so sensual.

"Are we there yet?"

Claire laughed and readjusted her hands on the steering wheel of the Jeep. "We've only been on the road fifteen minutes."

"Stop at the next gas station, will you? I want to get some munchies. Half the fun of cruising is the junk you eat on the way."

She pulled off at a tourist trap with a huge carved bear outside and real live geese waddling around on the porch, pooping all over everything.

She was standing in front of the soda case when Dylan motioned to her with one hand. "Come here. You've gotta check this out."

She went along with it until she reached the men's rest room. There she double-checked the sign.

"This is great," Dylan said, grabbing her by the elbow, trying to pull her inside. She looked behind her. Nobody around.

"This alone makes the day worthwhile," he said.

What could he possibly want her to see, she wondered, stepping inside.

He pointed proudly to the hand dryer on the wall.

"So?" she asked.

"Look closer."

Scratched in the paint were the words WIPE HANDS ON PANTIES.

"The message is getting out. I'll bet it says the same thing in the women's." He pushed her out the door, then went into the women's. He immediately returned to give her a wink and a thumbs up.

Oh, brother. She crossed her arms over her chest. "When I talked about showing you the sights, I didn't mean public rest rooms."

He grabbed her by both arms and gave her a firm, quick kiss, then let her go. "I appreciate your willingness to be flexible."

A lot of roads were closed because of the extreme amount of snow they'd had throughout the winter. But they were able to get to the waterfall by driving down a narrow canyon, then following the Salmon River for several miles.

Dylan made all the correct noises, the "Wows" and "That's amazings." But Claire had a feeling it didn't evoke the same sense of majesty she was feeling. And as they continued the drive, she came to realize that he didn't like the dark, confined areas, but he loved the lookout where you could stand on top of the world and see for hundreds of miles all the way across Hell's Canyon into Oregon.

She was glad they'd come. The outing gave Claire a new perspective on their relationship. And what she came away with was a realization of just how limited it was, and how little they knew about each other.

At the lookout, the air was cool, but the sun was warm on her face. "You should see this place in the spring and early summer," she said. "The wildflowers are unbelievable."

She'd mentioned the future. Would he have a response to that? Would he say, Let's come up here again then?

He didn't say anything. Instead, he seemed to be lost in his own reflective world.

Standing there, looking out across the huge expanse of wilderness and mountains served to remind Claire of how insulated their life together had become. She knew nothing about Dylan, nothing outside of who he was when he was at her house. There had been a couple of times when she'd tried to bring up the subject of his past, but he'd neatly sidestepped her question and turned the conversation another direction, into something funny, or something sexy. He certainly knew how to distract her.

"Have you ever seen the Grand Canyon?" he asked, finally breaking the almost religious silence.

"No."

"You should."

"There are a lot of things I want to see, places I want to go."

"Don't wait too long."

He seemed suddenly sad, depressed. She hadn't meant for the day to make him sad.

He kept his eyes focused on the horizon, where a lavender haze had settled between the peaks of tall pines. "I've been to a lot of places."

It was the first time he'd ever offered any information about himself. She was afraid to say anything, afraid he'd accidentally forgotten she was there, had accidentally spoken out loud.

"I've seen Kilimanjaro."

He turned to look over his shoulder at her, the wind ruffling what there was of his hair, his expression daring her to dispute what he'd just said. When she didn't, he continued. "I've seen the pyramids of Egypt." He shoved his hands into his pockets and hunched his back to the wind. "My parent were missionaries," he explained. The way he said it made her think that these were words he rarely spoke.

"That must have been wonderful. To go to so many places, see so many things."

"Yeah. Well." He turned back to stare out past the valley, to the blue, blue sky. "They were killed in an uprising in South Africa."

"Oh my God. Dylan. I'm so sorry." That explained a lot of things, like how he could be so intelligent, yet so directionless.

"I didn't tell you so you'd feel sorry for me. I hate that. Everybody has baggage. Some people just have a little more than others, that's all. Looking out there like this, well, it reminded me of those days, that's all."

He was so contemplative, so quiet. It was hard to believe that he was the same person who, just three hours earlier, had dragged her into the men's rest room so she could read the hand dryer.

He crouched down and placed his palm against the hard surface of the rock on which he stood. "You won't believe how hot this is. The winter solstice is over and the sun's really beginning to put out the heat." He ended up lying down on the rock, a hand behind his head. "Come here, Claire. You've got to feel the heat from this rock."

She joined him, kind of curled up next to

him, the heat from the rock radiating around them, the wind stinging their chilled faces. He closed his eyes and sighed. "I haven't felt this kind of freedom in years."

They lingered as long as they could, until the sun began to fade and darkness began to fall.

On the way home, Dylan discovered her stash of tapes in the glove compartment. "All right. Tunes." He began rummaging through the tapes. Some were old, some were fairly new. Libby, who liked nothing but Top Forty, was always complaining because Claire had such an odd assortment of tastes, the bands often groups Libby had never heard of. Claire's music preference changed with her mood, so her collection reflected a state of mind that was always fluctuating. She expected to hear the same complaint from Dylan that she heard from Libby.

She could see him out of the corner of her eye, reading first one tape, then another.

"All right. The Pixies," he said with satisfaction, bent over, reading by the tiny dim glow of the glove compartment light. "Frank Black's a genius when it comes to structured mayhem."

They hit a bump and he braced himself.

"Hey, Velvet Underground. They were ahead of their time, weren't they? Cowboy Junkies. This is the one they recorded in the church, isn't it?" He paused in his perusal and verbal cataloging, a tape in his hand. "You listen to Leonard Cohen?"

"He's a wonderful writer. You've heard of him?"

"Oh, yeah."

Judging from the reverent tone of his voice, it sounded as if Cohen's music had had an impact on Dylan's life.

He shut the glove compartment and took the tape from the case. "Does this have 'Suzanne' on it?"

"Side one, I think."

"This is so weird."

"What?"

"That you listen to Leonard Cohen."

"A lot of people think he's too sad, but I don't think his music's sad as much as—" She searched for a word.

"Spiritual?" Dylan offered, finishing her sentence.

"That's it. Spiritual."

He just kept holding the tape, staring at it. "I used to have a friend who liked Cohen," he finally said.

She got the idea it may have been something he didn't want to be reminded of, that it was maybe something too painful.

Olivia? She wondered. Had Olivia like Cohen?

Seeming to come to a decision, Dylan popped in the tape, then pushed buttons until he reached the song he was looking for.

"Stop the Jeep."

Claire braked, coming to a halt in the middle of the deserted road.

"Cut the lights."

Not sure of what he was after, she shut off the lights and the ignition.

Darkness had fallen. All the stars were out. Moonlight cast a shimmering trail along the road, like a path to heaven.

He pushed the PLAY button. The haunting, aching song filled the night, became a part of the moment. Claire stepped from the Jeep and just stood there, hands shoved deep into the pockets of her coat, looking up at the sky. Dylan came to stand beside her. And then, under a cobalt sky full of cadmium stars, he pulled her into his arms. Without a word, he kissed her, and rocked her against him, and just held her, as if he didn't want to let her go.

They stopped at a gas station along the Salmon River where Dylan picked up a newspaper.

"Isn't that the guy who was in the plane crash with you?" Claire asked, looking at the front page of the paper as he slid into the passenger seat. "The chess player?"

"Yeah. I guess he's winning all over the place. He's got a match scheduled with the guy who now holds the national championship."

"He must be really good."

"Yeah."

Although Dylan agreed, he sounded preoccupied.

She put the Jeep in gear and pulled back onto the highway. "Chess is cool."

"I always got the idea that most chicks thought it was nerdy."

"Oh, I don't know. When I was in high school, I used to know this guy who was on the school chess team. Of course everybody made fun of the kids on the team, but I actually thought there was something sexy about it."

"About *chess*?" he asked in total disbelief.

She laughed. "What's wrong with that?"

"Did you ever date the chess player?"

"No. He didn't date anybody, as far as I know."

"Would you have?"

"Dated him?"

"Yeah. Or would you have been embarrassed to be seen going into a theater with him? Or riding around in his geeky car?"

"I'd like to say I wouldn't have been embarrassed, but in all honesty, I may have been. We're talking about a sixteen-year-old here. That's one thing I regret about high school. I wish I'd stood up for what I believed in. I wasn't one of those clones who did everything everybody else was doing. But I didn't speak my mind, either."

"That's the easy thing to do. To watch it all go by."

"Let's talk about something a little more current."

"How about the chess thing?"

"That fascinates you, doesn't it?"

"I can't believe you think chess is sexy. Explain that one to me."

"I guess I'm turned on by intelligence. And people who play chess are smart."

"What if *I* played chess?"

She laughed. "*You?*"

"Yeah, me. What the hell are you laughing at?"

"It's just such a far-fetched premise."

"Oh, really?"

"Dylan, I didn't say that just because you *aren't* a chess player you don't turn me on."

"I'm glad we got that straightened out."

That night, they lay tangled together in bed, Claire's head against Dylan's shoulder. The day had been so much more than she'd expected.

Rather than going on an innocent drive, it had been a turning point in their relationship. Dylan had opened up to her, and she felt as if she understood him, while certainly not completely, at least a little bit, enough for her to feel she could ask a question that had been in her mind since they first met.

"Dylan . . . who is Olivia?"

She felt him tense, then relax.

"My sister," he finally said so quietly she barely heard him.

Claire lay there, stunned, silent.

"She died when I was twelve."

Oh, Dylan. I'm so sorry. So incredibly sorry.

Claire touched him, stroking his face, his hair.

The room was silent for a long time.

He made a throat-clearing sound. "After our parents died, I told her I'd take care of her. I guess I didn't do a very good job."

Her heart was breaking. She pressed her lips against his shoulder, unable to speak.

Twenty-four

Was it the voodoo doll?

No.

Yet Claire had to admit to herself that Dylan hadn't seemed the least attracted to her until she'd poked the doll with that last pin.

Too much of a coincidence?

Maybe. She hoped not. She *prayed* not.

There was one way to find out.

For the third time in a matter of hours, Claire opened the antique desk drawer and pulled out the Pillsbury Doughboy voodoo doll.

She grasped the white pin, but didn't pull it out. Just like she hadn't pulled it out the other times.

Tomorrow.

She'd do it tomorrow, she promised herself. One more day wouldn't make any difference. And really, when she thought about it, *two* more days wouldn't make any difference. Or three.

What you're doing is deceitful, said that

voice in her head she'd been trying hard to ignore.

"I *know,*" she told the Doughboy. She was an addict, and like all addicts, she kept putting off going to detox, kept putting off facing the inevitable.

I don't know that it's the doll.

There's only one way to find out.

"Tomorrow," she whispered to the little guy, giving him a kiss and tucking him gently into the drawer. "Tomorrow."

Dylan picked up a stick and gave it a toss in the direction of the house.

Hallie just smiled up at him, not even looking for the stick.

Dylan rubbed her soft head. "We can't all be geniuses."

If Claire was an addict, then Dylan was a junkie. He couldn't get enough of Claire. When he wasn't with her, he couldn't get her out of his mind. When he was with her, he couldn't believe his luck.

He was so damn confused. He'd never felt this way about a woman. In fact, there had been times when he'd wondered if he could have a real relationship with anyone. He'd wondered if the losses he'd suffered had screwed him up, turned him into some kind of robot, unable to feel deeply about anything. Over the years, he'd been with what he figured was probably an average number of women. And never had any of them touched him more than physically. Never had he felt that what they'd shared had been more than an act, more than a mutual . . . well, kind of handshake.

Two weeks had passed since the night Claire so inventively handcuffed herself to the bed. And in that time his passion for her hadn't diminished, not in the least. In fact, it was the opposite. And ever since that night, he noticed things in ways he'd never noticed them before. Colors were more intense. Smells were more exotic.

At the moment he noticed the way the cold air felt on a face that was hot from cutting wood. The way the ground felt under his feet. The way his body felt, kind of light, kind of electric.

He thought about the way Claire felt.

Soft. Sweet.

Unbelievable.

Things happened for a reason. He firmly believed that. Why else would his plane have crashed in the middle of the mountains? Why else would he have ended up getting into *Claire's* Jeep?

It seemed to be his destiny.

Cause and effect. Everything was connected. Even the death of his parents. That horrible night was the beginning of a journey, a journey that had been long and hard and painful. It was too bad people couldn't see into the future. If he'd known that Claire had been waiting somewhere up ahead, it would have made the hell he thought of as his life a lot easier to bear.

He moved in the direction of the house. He was trying to give Claire space so she could get some work done on her paintings, but it would be dark soon. From the end of the lane, he could see a light shining from the kitchen window, and he pictured Claire, curled up on the couch, sketchpad on her knee.

He moved toward that light.

Dylan came in from outside, Hallie at his heels, to find Claire sitting at the antique desk, a dreamy little smile hovering near the edges of her mouth. He crossed the room, took her face in his hands, and kissed her long and hard. It had been almost twenty-four hours since he'd held her close, skin to skin, soul to soul.

"Let's go outside in the sauna," he whispered, threading his fingers through her shiny hair.

"Don't you want to eat first? I made a casserole while you were gone."

"Later."

In truth, he was never hungry now. Who could be interested in food when there was Claire? Food was fuel, nothing more.

Outside in the sauna, they didn't even pretend that they were there for any other reason than to make love. They both quickly stripped.

"Wait," he said, putting a hand to hers as she started to pull off the bit of string she called underwear. "Let me."

He slipped his fingers under the elastic band, tracing it between her buttocks, then back to the soft mound of hair. He slid his hands beneath the elastic, then pulled the panties down her thighs and legs until she stepped free. He dropped to his knees, his hands kneading her bottom, her fingers digging into his hair, and he kissed her with his lips and his tongue. He loved the taste of her, the salty, erotic taste of her. Already he knew just where to touch her, just what it took to make her go weak. He dragged his tongue across that spot.

She let out a moan and slid to the floor so they were knee to knee, chest to chest.

"You know me so well," she said, her mouth finding his, her knee slipping between his thighs until she was riding him. "You know just where to touch me."

"You're almost there, aren't you?" he asked, newly amazed at how quickly she could reach an orgasm.

"*Yes.*" She let out a little gasping laugh. "I'm trying to hold back, trying to make this last, but I've been thinking about this moment all day."

"Why didn't you tell me earlier?"

"I was afraid you'd think I was some kind of maniac."

"We could have been maniacs together."

He lay her back on the wooden floor, taking

a moment to admire her glistening body, taking a moment to savor the heavy-lidded desire in her dark-pupiled eyes. He continued to watch her as she took him in her hands and guided him to her, continued to watch her as he filled her, continued to watch her as she met him, thrust for thrust, continued to watch her as she threw back her head and spasmed around him.

"Oh my," she said. "Oh my."

Claire didn't want to get up, didn't want to move, but she'd totally lost track of time. She had no idea whether or not they'd been inside the sauna too long. They had to get up. They had to get outside.

"We have to get up, " she said.

Dylan wouldn't move. Well, that wasn't quite true. He kind of moaned in a sleepy, contented way. He began to move his hips. She could feel him reawakening inside her. He pressed a hot, open-mouthed kiss against her neck and said her name over and over.

She slapped him on the arm, just a slight, open-hand kind of thing. "Dylan. We have to get out of here. Right now."

"Huh?"

"*Now.*"

It was with obvious great reluctance that he drew away from her. She was on her feet, picking up her clothes, when he grabbed her arm and tugged her in the direction of the door. "Forget your clothes."

They ran outside and tumbled into the snow. It felt cold and glorious against Claire's hot, hot skin. It had been twilight when they'd gone inside the sauna; now the darkness was complete, the moonlight reflecting off the snow making it easy to keep her bearings.

Laughing, Claire picked up a handful of snow and tossed it at Dylan's face. He grabbed first one of her arms, then the other. Then he slowly lowered himself on top of her—and filled her.

It was the strangest, most glorious feeling. The cold, the hot. *Dylan.*

"Are you too cold?" he asked, looking down at her.

She shook her head. "I'm so hot, the snow is melting around me."

He laughed, a breathless sound.

They came together, rolling and tumbling and breathless, until they were both depleted, until the cold air began to remind them both where they were. Dylan kissed her hard and rocked her against his chest, saying, "I think I'm in love."

Claire stopped breathing.

Love?

Under normal conditions, his sweet confession would have sent her blood singing. But all she could think about was the voodoo doll.

What if it wasn't real? What if he really didn't care anything for her?

"I guess that wasn't quite the news you wanted to hear." He moved away from her, got to his feet, walked back to the sauna. He returned, their clothes in his hand. He tossed hers at her, then disappeared into the house.

He hadn't meant to say anything. It certainly wasn't like him to blurt out declarations of love. And now that he thought about it, he hadn't actually said, I love you. He'd said, I *think* I'm in love. There was a big difference between the two, the latter giving him a way out.

By the time she showed up to eat, he'd recovered from the shock of his blunder and her subsequent rejection.

Claire sat at one end of the couch, her feet tucked under her, eating the tuna casserole she'd fixed earlier.

Did hers taste like sawdust too? Dylan wondered from where he sat in an overstuffed chair, his bare feet sticking out in front of him, plate in hand. "I didn't really mean it," he assured her. "I mean, I *like* you, of course. But I don't feel *that* way about you. It was just kind of an expression. Like saying, Wow."

She had no answer for him. She just kept staring at her plate, shoving in forkfuls of food as if eating was something she had to get done and over with in a hurry. Suddenly she jumped up and ran to the kitchen, plate in hand. He heard a cupboard door open, heard what sounded like the wastebasket being slid across the floor, then the sound of someone puking.

She could have just said she didn't think of him that way.

That night Dylan didn't sleep in her bed. Claire stayed awake, staring into the darkness above her head, waiting until she heard the sound of his even breathing.

That didn't happen until after three in the morning.

She tossed back the covers, then tiptoed into the living room. Once there, she slowly pulled open the desk drawer, wincing at every little sound.

"Claire?" came Dylan's sleepy voice out of the darkness. "That you?"

"Yes," she whispered, her heart pounding, her fingers wrapped around the stuffed doll. "I didn't mean to wake you. I'm just looking for something."

"Did you find it?"

She closed the drawer and clutched the doll tightly to her chest. "Yes. Yes, I found it."

Back in the bedroom, under the moonlight streaming in the window, Claire pulled out first one pin, then the other, dropping the pins in the wastebasket near the bed.

What was she supposed to do with the doll now? she wondered. Should she take off the hair she'd glued to it? What if that had some negative effect on Dylan? And she certainly couldn't throw it away, certainly couldn't risk damaging the doll in any way. Who did a person get in contact with about such things? Was there a voodoo hotline? Maybe the library could help her find a voodoo expert, someone who could tell her how to deactivate the doll.

For the time being she put it in her top dresser drawer for safekeeping. If it were the voodoo doll that had made Dylan fall in love with her, then when he woke up in the morning, she would be old Mrs. Mothballs again.

I think I'm in love.

And she'd told herself one more day wouldn't make any difference.

Twenty-five

The next morning, Dylan stuffed his last shirt into the black plastic trash bag, pulled the yellow strings tight, and knotted them. He'd waited until Claire got up, waited until she was out of the bedroom before packing his stuff.

Becoming famous was like winning the lottery. Suddenly you had a lot of friends, people who wouldn't have looked at you twice before. He hadn't told Claire who he was because he wanted to make sure she liked *him*, Dylan, not the chess player. He'd almost told her that day they'd gone for a drive, but then she'd brought up all that stuff about how she was attracted to chess players, and all of his old insecurities had come tumbling back. He'd decided then and there that he had to find out how she felt about him first, before he told her who he was. That was the only way he could be certain of her true feelings. He just hadn't bargained on her not *having* any feelings for him.

He was stunned. He was hurt.

And now he thought, To hell with telling her anything.

"Wow."

He turned to see Claire standing in the doorway.

He looked around the room, making sure he had everything. "Why wow?"

"That was fast. One day you're staying, the next you're leaving."

"I've been thinking about it quite a while."

"What made you choose today? Just the day after you said you loved me?"

"Claire, let's get this straight." His pride had suffered. He couldn't leave with her thinking he was running away, that she'd broken his heart or something. "I said I *think* I'm in love. That's different. And don't worry. I was just caught up in the passion of the moment. That's what it's called, isn't it? The passion of the moment? It didn't mean anything. It was like yelling, All right. Touchdown!"

She flinched, and he instantly regretted the callousness of his words. But it was too late. Once spoken, words couldn't be taken back.

He couldn't stay. That was all he knew. Here he thought he'd found the person he'd been searching for his entire life. But it was like everything else that had ever happened to him. He found the promise of happiness, only to have it taken away.

"Are you leaving because of yesterday?"

She came and stood directly in front of him, demanding an answer. For a moment he was afraid she was going to block his way. He didn't know what he'd do if she blocked his way. Because at the moment, he was close to breaking down, close to falling apart there at her feet, dangerously close to confessing his damn love, his damn, damn love all over again.

"I'm an ass." He wasn't sure where that had come from, but it was a good diversion for both of them.

"W-What?" She looked at him as if she couldn't have heard right.

He strode past her, pushing her a little as he went, but not much.

"Dylan, you don't have to leave. This isn't a big deal."

He made it through the living room, almost to the front door before he stopped. She was right behind him. Without looking back, he said, "No, it isn't. No big deal at all."

Did it matter? Did any of it really matter? He'd never been one to feel sorry for himself. Everybody had baggage. Hell, to not have baggage would be to have baggage.

"Where are you going?"

"I have to see somebody."

"What about prison? You're a wanted man. If they catch you, you'll be in ten times the trouble. Why don't you turn yourself in? I have a friend who knows a good lawyer."

He swung around, his gaze only a little blurry. "Listen," he said, his voice loud, angry, a calming contrast to the ache in his chest. It didn't matter. None of it mattered. Hadn't he already lived a thousand lifetimes? And weren't a thousand lifetimes too much for one person? "Why don't you just forget you ever met me? Why don't you just pretend I don't exist?"

She bit her bottom lip, and for the briefest of seconds, he thought *she* was going to cry, but it had to be a trick of the light. "But you *do* exist," she said, putting a nervous hand to her chest, pulling at one of the buttons there.

No, that's where she was wrong. He didn't exist. He hadn't existed for years and years and years. He'd just been a shadow, moving through the days, taking up time and space, wasting oxygen. Except for the brief days when Claire, his sweet, sweet Claire, had breathed life into him.

It suddenly occurred to him that he was like a locust that remains underground in a suspended state for twenty years only to emerge for a few brief days. Uriah would have appreciated that analogy.

"Bye, Claire. It's been—" He was about to say fun, but that didn't quite convey the triteness he was after. "Interesting. It's been interesting."

That finally got to her.

"Okay, go! Just *go*."

She pointed toward the door, toward something out there in the distance, some other state, some other country. "I'll forget about you in a second. In half a second. You were just a guy who kidnapped me."

He was sorry about that.

"Who held me at gunpoint."

Sorry about that, too.

She put a hand to her forehead. "What could I have been thinking?" she asked herself, her voice thick with disbelief. She sounded as if she'd completely forgotten how this had all started. "I get it now," she said, again to herself, her voice growing stronger as her apparent ability to reason returned. "It's like the Patty Hearst thing." She plopped down on a chair at the table, her eyes distant, focusing on something in her thoughts, something that finally made sense.

"She was kidnapped, and abused, but then she actually ended up succumbing to her captors. She actually ended up *joining* them." Elbows on the table, she dug her fingers through her hair. "And look what I've done. I've harbored a criminal! My God!" She pressed a hand to her mouth, staring straight ahead in horror. She looked up at him, then spoke slowly, painfully. "I had sex with you."

"I never forced you. You know damn well I never forced you." This was getting so fucking ugly. He should leave, just walk away, but he couldn't make himself. Not yet.

"No." She let out a self-deprecatory sort of laugh. "I'll take the blame for that. It was entirely my fault. That's what is so inexcusable about this whole thing. *I* seduced *you*. You really weren't interested in me at all."

"That's not true." Don't do this.

"No, you weren't."

"I was." *I am.*

She sat back in her chair, arms crossed. "I should call the cops."

"What?"

"The cops. I should call the cops and tell them you're here. Tell them you're alive."

"Don't do that."

"No. I won't. I couldn't."

"At least you don't hate me that much." How had this happened? *How did we get like this?* He'd told her he might love her, and everything fell apart. How had a few innocent, honest words turned everything upside down?

She got to her feet. She came to stand in front of him. She took his hand. She lifted it to her face, to her cheek. A tear dampening his knuckle. "I'm sorry. It's not your fault."

She dropped his hand and turned her back to him. "Have you ever noticed how people spend so much of their adult lives trying to recapture a little piece of their childhood? Maybe they move to a town that reminds them of the place where they grew up. Or maybe they see a house that reminds them of a special place where they used to play. Or a neighborhood. Or maybe a feeling."

He heard her pull in a deep, shaky breath, then continued. "I had this storybook childhood. I mean, it's almost embarrassing, it was so perfect. Then my mother died and my father remarried and they had kids. And life was okay. It wasn't terrible, by any means. But for some reason, it made everything that had happened before my dad remarried into a kind of sham. Because his new wife, she was real. And his new kids, they were real. I was a part of the old life, a part of the past."

"And what have you been looking for, Claire?" he asked quietly.

"Perfect love. The kind of love I felt when I was a child."

But he wasn't the one, obviously. And last night, his blunt confession had made her realize that.

She turned around. She attempted to smile up at him through her tears. "Whenever I see a hand dryer with the words 'Wipe Hands on Panties,' I'll think of you."

"Anytime I see one of your cards, I'll think of you." Or a black winter sky full of brilliant stars. Or snow. Or pine trees. Or birds. Or frogs. Or grasshoppers. Or—

"Bye," she said.

"Yeah, bye."

She stood at the door and watched him go, watched until his car disappeared, watched until the sound of the engine faded into the distance.

Hallie made a whining sound, and sat down beside her, leaning against Claire's leg, as if needing to feel the comfort of a human body.

He was just some guy who'd kidnapped her, she reminded herself, reaching to pet Hallie. He was just some guy who'd made love to her. He was just some guy who'd broken her heart.

It was easier for the person who was leaving. He could start over. But for the person left behind. . . . Everything was a reminder.

In the bedroom, she opened the top drawer of her dresser and pulled out the voodoo doll. It was so tempting.

All she would have to do would be to stick a couple of pins there . . . and he would turn around. He would come flying back.

"You surprised me," she told the doll. "I really didn't believe in you. I really expected him to be in love with me." She held the doll in both hands, and for a brief moment she wanted to give it a shake. But then she remembered what she was dealing with, and just how much power it had.

Enough to make a man fall in love with a woman. Enough to make him desire her so much that he couldn't think of anything else.

That was some voodoo. Some wonderful voodoo.

Twenty-six

Dylan didn't make it far. Five miles from Fallon, his generator light came on. By the time he got to Jim's Garage, a short had burned out the car's regulator and generator.

"It could take a week to ten days," Jim said, as he wiped grease from his hands with a red rag, acting as if a week to ten days was a good thing.

What difference did it make? Dylan thought. He didn't know where he was going, didn't have any plans. Maybe this was one of those neon signs that showed up in his life from time to time. Maybe he was supposed to stay put.

He ended up checking into The Haven, a cheap motel on the edge of town. He liked it because it was set back under a bunch of pine trees and you couldn't really see it from the road. Plus, it didn't look like anybody else was staying there.

He checked in, tossed his black plastic bag on the bed, called Zeke, and asked him to find a phone number.

* * *

After making it big, Dylan could have taken his money and moved to some Mediterranean island off the coast of Spain. Instead, he moved to Pretty, a little town in the Arizona desert just off a stretch of abandoned highway ten miles from the Mexican border. There he became a pump jockey at a mom and pop gas station/grocery store. Pretty wasn't really a town at all anymore, and Dylan just figured the word "abysmal" had fallen from the bottom of the welcome sign years ago.

The only things left in Pretty—or Purty, as he later discovered it was pronounced—were tumbleweeds and fence after fence of hubcaps the owner and his wife had collected over the years. There wasn't much business, just the occasional family on its way to or from California. Maybe their van broke down. Maybe they just stopped to take a gander at the dump. And it was a dump. Jimmy LaRoache collected things. Toilets—he must have had forty of them. Cars— maybe fifty. Gas pumps—a hundred? The LaRoaches, bless their hearts, weren't advocates of *feng shui*.

Dylan lived in one of the half-dozen green, shingle-sided shanties that used to be part of a motel business. Twenty steps from his front door was a swimming pool that hadn't seen water in fifteen years. The faded, mint-green bottom was covered with weeds and tires and trash that had blown in from hundreds of miles away. But in his room, Dylan had a television hooked up to a giant satellite dish.

What more did a guy need?

Dylan hadn't gone to Pretty looking for a job. It was just another one of those neon signs that had a way of popping into his life. He'd been driving around, just driving, trying to find a place that could be termed "middle of nowhere," and feeling he was getting damn close, when he stopped for gas and nobody came out to wait on him. His tank was almost empty, and, according to the map, the next town was ninety miles away.

He found the owner watching TV in one of the little motel rooms, one bare foot propped on a pillow, nursing a case of the gout. His wife had gone to the nearest town to get some kind of salve, whatever salve was.

Jimmy—the owner's name turned out to be Jimmy—handed Dylan the key to the gas pump, told him to fill his tank and come back with the money.

Dylan filled up, returned with the key and money, and offered to stay and help out for nothing.

"Have any experience?" Jimmy asked.

"I can take a tire off a rim in less than a minute." His time with Uncle Hank hadn't been entirely wasted.

"You're hired."

For a while, Dylan loved it. Nobody following him. Nobody shoving cameras in his face. Nobody acting as if they were best buddies when they weren't. He had a satellite dish, and later the Internet.

He was one happy puppy.

On Sundays, the Missus—Jimmy called his wife "the Missus," which Dylan thought was better than "the little woman." Anyway, on Sundays, she had card club and a bunch of her friends would come over and play pitch and rummy. Sometimes Dylan joined them, much to their delight.

Occasionally, Dylan would drive to the nearest town some ninety miles away where he would drink beer, get laid, and fight.

But as the months wore on—turning into years, much to his numb surprise—a restlessness began to grow in him. He was ready to move on, but the LaRoaches were in bad health.

That was about the time their daughter got a divorce and moved back home. Dylan thought it was his chance to get away, but Harriet immediately made it clear to him that she wanted him in her bed, so he stayed on a while longer.

Sex with Harriet was okay. It certainly broke up the monotony of the days, but then she began pressuring him to marry her.

Sex with Harriet was one thing, holding a conversation quite another. And *marrying* her, well, that was out of the question.

The marriage issue became a turning point in Dylan's career of self-imposed exile. He had to take a step back and reevaluate his life, ask himself where the hell this was going.

He had things to do. Places to go.

Snow. He wanted to see snow. He wanted to touch snow. He was sick of the desert. He wanted to experience a change of seasons. He was thirty years old, and he couldn't imagine weather so cold that it could actually kill a person.

"You ever seen snow, Harriet?"

"Snow?" She lit a cigarette and blew out the match. "Sure, I seen snow," she said, her nasal twang annoying him more than usual. "I hate it."

"What's it like?"

"Like? Well, it's cold, sugar. Real cold. Cold enough to freeze the balls off a brass monkey." She giggled, getting as much of a kick out of her own joke as if she'd come up with it herself.

I've got to get out of here, Dylan thought.

The opportunity presented itself the very next day. He was checking out the Internet and decided to type in his own name to see if the buzz about him had died down. Daniel French. Dylan was his middle name, the name his parents had called him, and Olivia had called him, and Uriah. Dylan was a name from his past.

There were Daniel French websites out the ying-yang, a lot of them with huge, full-screen photographs. And as he looked at the photos, he noticed something. In nine years, a person's looks could really change. He'd hardly been more than a kid when he'd decided to drop out of sight. In those last pictures, he'd been gangly and pale, with hardly enough facial hair to shave. Nowadays, after a few hours, he needed to shave again. Hair that used to be light brown was now dark. Eyes that used to be brown were hazel, faded by the intense desert sun. No longer skinny and gangly, Dylan's chest had broadened, his arms doubled in size.

If he returned to civilization, would people put it together? Would they see any similarity between the boy he used to be and the man he'd become?

Dylan went back to the search engine screen and typed in the word CHESS. He spent about three hours going to different websites before stumbling across a buried site containing a couple of obscure lines about a guy named Trevor Davis, who had learned to play chess while doing time in prison. Even though it was an abandoned site, there was a photo of the guy.

The weird thing was, Trevor Davis looked like an older version of the young Dylan. His hair was light brown, his eyes dark. He was a little on the thin side.

That night, Dylan couldn't sleep. More than anything, he craved anonymity. He wanted to be able to go to a baseball game without being hounded. He wanted to be able to go to a movie, go out to eat. He wanted to *see* things, go places. This wasn't living. He was just as much a prisoner in his own house as Trevor Davis had been in prison.

He had to find this guy, this Davis. And when he found him, he would ask him if he wanted to be famous for fifteen minutes.

The big neon sign was pointing again, telling him to find Davis, that the guy could be the solution he was seeking.

And when he found him, and if Davis agreed to help, he would let the press know that Daniel French was coming out of retirement. Then Davis would take Dylan's place. He would come forward and play a big chess game. Davis's photo would be splashed on every newspaper and every tabloid, every TV screen in the world. And then Davis would lose the game, and disappear. And Dylan would be a free man.

It had seemed so simple, so straightforward, so perfect. Dylan, whose working life had been a series of strategies, hadn't taken into account the possibility of unknown factors.

Like a plane crash.

And Davis himself.

And Claire. Claire had come out of nowhere, blindsiding him.

In his room at The Haven, Dylan tucked the receiver under his chin and dialed the number he'd gotten from Zeke, almost expecting to hear himself answer.

He heard a click, followed by a guy's voice.

"Is Mr. French there?" Dylan asked.

"Speaking."

"Daniel Dylan French?"

"Yes."

"This is just weird as hell."

"Who is this?"

"You and I have the *exact* same name. Now what are the odds against that? I could see if my name was Mr. Smith, and your name was Mr. Smith. But Daniel Dylan French. That's odd. That's just odd as hell, don't you think?"

At the other end, there was silence. Then, finally, "Daniel?"

"I prefer Dylan, but you wouldn't know that."

"My God. I thought you were dead!"

Dylan could almost visualize Davis's mouth hanging open, visualize the poor guy trying to figure out how to get out of this one.

"Tell me, Davis. Did you have this whole thing planned from the beginning? Were you going to kill me, dump my body somewhere, then become me?"

"No. Shit, no. Do you think I planned the crash? That would have been suicidal. But then, when we did crash— At first I thought you were dead. I really thought you were dead and I was the only survivor. And we already had every-thing set up. The identity switch. How could I *not* go through with it? It was too perfect."

"There was just one thing wrong," Dylan pointed out. "Two, actually. I wasn't dead, and you forgot to mention that you still had a couple years' hard time hanging over your head."

"I'm glad you're not dead. I never wanted you to be dead. I've always been a big fan of yours."

"Don't bullshit me."

"I'm not."

"You've been busy being me."

"I did what I was supposed to do, which was pretend to be you. That was the deal."

"The deal was, you were supposed to play one game of chess, and *lose*."

Davis laughed, apparently over the initial shock of hearing Dylan's voice. "I told you I was good, but you didn't believe me. I have to admit that pissed me off. Do you think you're the only person in the world who can play chess?"

"You're such a con. You're so full of shit."

"What do you want? Do you want your identity back? It sucks that I've been winning all over the place and I'm using somebody else's name. But I'm in too deep. I don't want to do any more time. I won't. I can't go back there. You've got to have some idea how it would be in prison for a guy like me. And now it's like I'm somebody else. That prison stuff—it's like remembering a movie I watched a long time ago, a movie I didn't like, a movie that made me sick." His voice dropped. "I can't go back there. Don't make me go back there."

Dylan felt sorry for him, but not that sorry. Davis had left him in the mountains to die. He'd given Dylan a past he didn't want. "It wasn't exactly an even exchange," Dylan said. "Grand master for grand theft."

"I'm sorry, man. What do you want from me?"

"How good are you?" Dylan asked.

"What?"

"Chess. Are you really good, or are you such a sham, such a con artist that you throw your opponent off? Or is it the name? I remember when it got to the point where my name alone was winning games. People froze. They couldn't function and they did stupid things. Is that the way it is with you, Davis? Or should I call you Dylan? But then, you prefer Daniel, if I remember right."

"What do you *want*?" The guy's voice was rising in panic. Dylan could almost hear the sweat rolling off him.

"I want to know how good you are."

"I'm good. I told you, I'm good."

"As good as I am?"

"Yeah, maybe. I play a lot like you."

"I'll bet you do. It wouldn't do to have someone mention the French Capture or Daniel's Legacy and not know what they were. You have to have copied my style, otherwise people would be suspicious."

"I know everything there is to know about

you. I know that you prefer the romantic school of Adolf Anderssen and Paul Murphy to Karpov."

He was right. Dylan had admired the romantic style because of its free-spirited takes and quest for beauty. Chess wasn't supposed to be sterile. It was supposed to be a dance. A sweetly choreographed dance. Poetry. Dylan laughed. "You're so damn cocky."

"You asked me if I was good. Yeah, I'm good. As good as you." There was a thoughtful pause. "Maybe better."

"Then play me."

"What?"

"I'm challenging you to a game of chess."

Twenty-seven

Someone was knocking at the door.

Claire wrapped her pillow around her head, shoving it against her ears. *Go away.*

But the knocking kept on and on.

Finally it stopped. *Thank God.*

That small moment of silence was followed by the sound of a key being slid into a lock, the sound of the door being swung open.

Claire dropped the pillow and sat up in bed, listening to a booted footfall approaching.

Dylan?

Libby's head appeared around the corner. "My God," she said as soon as she saw Claire. "You look like shit."

Claire tried to tuck a lank strand of hair behind her ear. It drooped forward. Even her hair was in mourning. And then she realized it was practically the middle of the night. "What are you doing here?"

"I'm sorry." Libby put her hands in the air.

"You know I don't barge in on people like this, but I saw your boyfriend in town and wondered if everything was okay."

"He's not my boyfriend."

"Well whatever he is, I saw him yesterday and said hi, and he didn't even know I was there. Is he on drugs? I hope you aren't dating somebody who's on drugs."

"We aren't dating."

"Then I saw him again tonight. He was at The Brewery using the phone. I just happened to be coming out of the rest room. He was calling a taxi to take him to the airport."

"He was catching a plane out of here. What's so unusual about that? Libby, you're letting your paranoia loose again."

"I'm not done. Just the day before, I was talking to Craig, the private pilot Craig, and he said he'd gotten a call to fly to Boise and pick up somebody."

"Is this going anywhere?"

"This person asked Craig if he could fly instrument, because he had to land here in the middle of the night, tonight. Craig was going to turn it down, but the guy was paying big bucks and he couldn't refuse."

"What does this have to do with Dylan?"

"This mystery guy must be the person Dylan is meeting at the airport. Claire, is he in some kind of trouble?"

Trouble? Dylan?

Those two words just naturally went together.

Claire tumbled out of bed and began pulling on clothes. She wasn't sure what desperate business Dylan used to be involved in, but it sounded like he was picking up where he'd left off.

"Claire, what the hell is going on? I mean, Dylan seemed like a nice guy. You two looked good together. Now he looks like hell, and you look like hell, and it sounds like he's running drugs or something."

"I'm afraid you might be right."

Claire pulled her hair back from her face. "Oh God." She had to talk to somebody. She had to tell Libby what was going on.

Claire dropped to the bed. "You aren't going to believe this."

She told Libby everything, beginning with the kidnapping and going to the handcuffs and the voodoo doll. Libby's jaw just kept dropping.

When Claire was finished, she got to her feet and hurried to the living room to find her boots, Libby hurrying behind her, for once too stunned for words. "Did he say what motel?" Claire asked, shoving her foot into a boot, hopping around, finding the other boot, quickly lacing both of them up. "When? Where?" Didn't he have any sense? Just a few days away from her sight and he was already getting himself into trouble.

"The Haven."

"That dive?"

"They were meeting at one A.M. And you know what my mother always said when I wanted to stay out past curfew: Nothing good ever happens after ten o'clock."

Claire checked the wall clock. It was almost one now.

Dylan sat facing Davis, a card table between them, the chess pieces lined up on the board, the clock to his left.

"I remember when you came out of nowhere and played that Russian in Leningrad before it became Saint Petersburg," Davis said. "They called you the Dark Horse. How old were you then? Seventeen? Eighteen?"

"Eighteen."

That seemed so long ago. It was a time when all Dylan was concerned with was the game. That's all that mattered to him. So innocent. So naïve. He didn't know that winning the game had a price, and that price was loss of personal freedom. It was funny, the way Davis didn't want to go back to prison, and yet he was heading straight for another kind of confinement. But some people were showmen. They didn't mind that their lives were played out on a public field. Dylan had the feeling Davis would thrive on such an existence.

Dylan dug a quarter out of the front pocket of his jeans. "We'll flip for color."

The motel was dim and stale, smelling of damp carpet and mildew and the lingering odor of a thousand people who'd passed through the seedy room. In one corner was a hanging lamp attached to a gold chain, on the bed a spread of avocado-green chenille.

Davis looked about like Dylan remembered him. The glasses. The thin face, thin arms poking out below short white sleeves. On the airplane, before the crash, they had joked that Davis looked the part of the chess player, Dylan the part of an ex-con.

Davis called it. Dylan flipped the coin, caught it, and slapped it down on his forearm. "Looks like you get white."

Davis straightened his pieces. "I can't believe I'm playing you. I used to dream about playing you."

Dylan wouldn't admit it to Davis, but for the first time in years, he was looking forward to playing, he was actually feeling a tense excitement. And also anxiety. Could he beat him? Playing chess wasn't like riding a bike. It wasn't something you could just walk away from, then take up again without practice, without conditioning yourself like any athlete.

A game of the mind, yes, but there were so many more things involved, so many more elements, so many layers.

Dylan was stale. Dylan was out of shape. Christ, he hadn't played in years.

Could he win?

Probably not. But he was getting off on the challenge.

Davis opened by moving his pawn to occupy the center, opening lines for the queen and bishop to move out of the back rank. The Ruy Lopez Opening?

Dylan mimicked Davis's move.

Davis brought his knight into play, threatening Dylan's central pawn.

Dylan had read that Davis was a master of the end game. A lot of people thought the end game was the only really important part of chess. They didn't try to memorize beginnings, or middles, but instead focused all of their attention on mastering the end game.

Over the years, Dylan had come to realize that if you wanted to play with the big boys, you had to be strong at the beginning, the middle, and the end. He'd also taught himself to diversify his openings, his objective always being one of surprise and originality.

In a few moves, it became apparent that Davis was like so many people Dylan had played over the years. He'd memorized the plays, and, like so many dedicated players, he didn't play from his heart, his soul, his gut. Davis saw the board as a puzzle to solve, not a battle to be won. He didn't see it as a dance. He didn't see the poetry. The beauty.

Davis was good.

He was damn good.

But he wasn't great. He wasn't grand master material. Which wasn't saying that he couldn't be someday. With the proper coaching. It would take a lot of unlearning, a lot of deprogramming, but it could be done.

"You just fell for a poison pawn."

"I saw it."

But Dylan knew he hadn't.

There were even a couple of moments when Davis surprised him. And there was a brief move that even hinted at a promise of brilliance. But Davis wasn't the challenge Dylan had hoped for. That sad fact quickly became apparent to Davis himself.

When the game was over, Davis sat staring at the board. He finally reached across the table and shook Dylan's hand. "Thanks. You've taught me a valuable lesson."

Dylan actually felt sorry for him. He'd had such big hopes, big dreams, only to come to a dingy motel in Fallon, Idaho, to find out he just didn't have what it took.

"You're good," Dylan told him, hoping their game together wouldn't turn him away from chess completely.

Davis shook his head. "Not nearly as good as I thought I was."

"You were nervous. Maybe feeling a little intimidated."

Again Davis shook his head and let out a harsh laugh. "I thought I could beat you."

"You play too much from here." Dylan pointed to his forehead.

"That's been my strength. My ability to memorize plays."

"So I noticed. But if that's all you ever do, then you're never playing your own game. You have to play your own game. Give yourself a chance."

"Think you'll ever go back?"

Dylan picked up the black knight and turned it around in his hand. He loved the way a good chess piece felt, the weight of it, the balance. "I think about it sometimes. But there doesn't seem to be any way to separate the game from all the garbage that goes with it. All I ever cared about was the game."

His own words took him by surprise, because there had been a time when Dylan didn't even care about the game anymore. When he'd felt like the hired assassin he told Claire he was, when winning had become no more than a calculated kill. Why was it that when one part of your life seemed to get better, the other part collapsed? Was that some kind of rule?

"Have you ever been in love?" Dylan asked. "Really in love?" Dylan didn't know where that had come from. Maybe it was the lateness of the night that had brought about such a personal question.

Dylan could see that it took Davis by surprise. Davis motioned to himself. "I look like this, and I play chess. What do you think?"

"I'm talking love of the unrequited kind."

Davis smiled. "*That*, my friend, I know. That I understand."

Ah. So they had more in common than chess and switched identities.

"How about some coffeehouse chess?"

"That sloppy shit?"

"That's your problem, Davis. Chess is supposed to be *fun*, not work." And in so saying, Dylan realized that that was exactly what he himself had lost sight of.

It didn't take Claire long to decide that if Dylan was up to something illegal, then somebody needed to stop him before he got into any more trouble.

Claire took the gun, unloaded of course, and tucked it into the front of her jeans the way Dylan had carried it. At the last minute, she tossed the Pillsbury Doughboy into her purse. You never knew when some voodoo might come in handy.

In summer, The Haven was always booked solid, dive though it was. In winter, it was almost deserted. If someone needed a hotel, they could be choosy. The only people who used The Haven in winter were a few hookers, people involved in affairs, and criminals. None of the categories were particularly impressive.

"Looks like we found the town's hot spot,"

Libby said in a low voice as Claire pulled off the road and parked near the office.

The motel was long and narrow, with a dozen orange doors that opened onto the parking lot.

"Now what?" Claire asked, realizing that they had no plan.

"We need to figure out which room is his and get the key. If nobody's there, we'll go in and look around."

"You're enjoying this, aren't you?" Claire asked, reaching for the doorhandle.

Libby just grinned. She was in her element.

Libby waited in the Jeep while Claire took on the task of obtaining the room key. In the office, she came upon two teenagers making out in front of the television.

She made a throat-clearing sound.

Nothing happened.

She tried again, thinking that she might have to get a hose pretty soon.

The pair reluctantly separated, the male of the duo getting to his feet and making his way to the cracked countertop.

"I need another key to my room," Claire said, eyeing the row of keys dangling from little gold hooks on a pegboard wall.

"What's your number?" the kid asked, rubbing his belly. He was groggy-looking, his clothes twisted, his hair sticking straight up.

"Uh . . ."

The kid stood there, bored, anxious to get back to more important business.

She checked out the row of keys. "I can't remember. Could you look in your book?"

The guest register was lying on the counter. With an irritated sigh, the kid flipped open the book.

Claire's gaze quickly fell to the page with its list of names. Nobody named Dylan. Of course she wouldn't have expected him to go by his real name. If that was his real name. "We've been here a few days . . ." she said vaguely.

"Mr. Black."

Mr. Black? That was a little like Mr. Green. Or Professor Plum. Yes, it was done in the motel room, with the revolver, by Mr. Black.

"Room six." He grabbed a key and slid it across the counter, then returned to his make-out session.

Claire snatched up the gold-colored key with its diamond-shaped plastic tag and hurried from the lobby before someone with authority showed up. Thank God for rude, lazy teenagers. And thank God for motels that didn't believe in updating their lock system for the safety of their patrons.

As soon as she stepped out the door, Libby jumped from the Jeep and ran over to her. "Get it?" she asked in a loud whisper.

Claire nodded and looked down the row of rooms. Number six was the only room with a light.

They approached the door, stopping outside.

Claire stood there. This was stupid. What was she doing? What if Libby was wrong?

Claire grabbed Libby's arm and pulled her back several steps from the room. "What if he's in there with some woman? What if they're in bed?"

"So?"

"*So?* My God, Libby."

"Come on." Libby dragged Claire back to the room, then put her ear to the door.

Claire watched her friend's face, the questioning eyebrows, the distant stare, and put her own ear to the door.

The first voice she heard was one she didn't recognize. "You can't quit when you're one of the best. I remember how, after you pulled that job in Russia, people started calling you the Hit Man."

"I don't want to talk about me." Dylan's voice.

"Okay, but I didn't come here to prove I could replace you. I came here to talk you into coming back."

"I'm not going back."

Claire silently handed the key to Libby.

"Then I can't be here," the stranger said. "I can't do this."

"No!" came Dylan's voice through the door. "Don't!"

Libby unlocked the door, Claire pulled out her gun—and fell inside the room.

Twenty-eight

The motel room door flew open.

Dylan looked up from the chessboard to see Claire stumble in, gun in hand.

Her eyes went from him, to Davis, then back to him.

Busted.

Davis jumped to his feet, hands high, chess pieces scattering.

Staring at the woman he loved, a woman who had rejected that love, Dylan asked, "Is this a raid?"

"You're playing chess?"

The incredulous expression on Claire's face was something he didn't think he'd ever forget.

He was so damn glad to see her, even if she was pointing a gun at him. "It may seem like a harmless pastime," he said, "but you know what they say. First it's chess, then it's the hard stuff."

Standing near the open door, Libby let out an unladylike snort.

"But I heard you shout."

"He was going to put away the pieces before the game was over."

Claire tossed the gun on the bed, the weapon bouncing. She dropped to her knees and began crawling around, picking up chess pieces. She had to hide. She had to distract herself. "I didn't know you were playing chess. I thought there was some kind of drug deal going down. Or some kind of hit being planned."

Keeping her face hidden, she lifted her hand and felt around until her knuckles came in contact with the surface of the table. She let go of five chess pieces, then went searching for more.

Dylan joined her under the table.

She couldn't look at him. "This is so embarrassing."

"I'm finding it rather enlightening. And very entertaining. Things were getting a little boring around here, isn't that right, Davis?"

"Uh, right," came a man's flustered voice from above the table. "Is this a bust or not?"

"This is that unrequited business."

"Oh . . . ?" That was followed by a thoughtful pause. "Oh."

Dylan picked up the queen. "You know . . ." He kind of bounced the piece in his hand, as if testing its weight. "I used to like the knight best, but now I think the queen is my favorite piece." He reached above his head and put it back on the table. *"J'aboube."*

Dylan's chess partner burst out laughing, as if it was the funniest thing he'd ever heard. *"J'aboube,"* Dylan repeated. "It means, I adjust. You're supposed to say it before you straighten a piece."

"Oh." How on earth would she have known that?

Dylan's friend was still laughing, and Claire was beginning to feel more stupid by the second.

"Even if there was a drug deal going down, what are you doing here? Have you suddenly joined the weekend police?"

"No, I— Well, I didn't want to see you get into any more trouble than you're already in."

He stopped her hands in their frantic search for more pieces. *"Why?"*

"Well . . . I . . ."

"Claire?"

Dylan reached for her, tilting up her face until she was looking at him in the dark under the table. "I thought you hated me."

"I never hated you. How could you think I hate you?"

He was looking at her as if he wanted to kiss her. He would kiss her, if she let another second go by. "I have to go." She backed out from under the table, bumping her head as she stood up.

Claire wanted to disappear, to vanish. Now that she was upright, she took better note of the other man in the room. While he no longer stood with his hands in the air, he nonetheless had his back to the wall, staring at her as if she were crazy. He might be onto something.

"Do I know you?" she asked. He looked familiar. "Aren't you the chess player?"

The man shot a nervous glance in Dylan's direction, then quickly shook his head.

"Yes you are. Daniel French. That's your name. You're Daniel French."

Dylan took a step toward her. "Claire, we have to talk."

What was going on here? She turned to see Libby still standing near the door with her fingers pressed hard to her lips, her eyes glistening, trying to hold back her hysteria.

Claire had to get away. She was so ashamed. Of everything. "Go ahead and laugh," she said to her friend, completely humiliated. "This was your bright idea." How had she let herself become involved in Libby's paranoia? She should have known better. Claire edged past her, stepping out into the cold night.

"But it's funny!" Libby shouted after her.

She wasn't quite sure why, but Claire felt like the victim of some stupid prank. Without waiting for Libby to catch up, Claire jumped into the Jeep and turned the key. The passenger door opened and closed.

Lost in her misery, Claire backed up, then began to pull out of the parking lot.

"You can't say you don't hate me," Dylan said from the passenger seat, "then take off like that."

Claire slammed on the brakes, almost sending them both through the windshield. She put the Jeep in neutral and pulled out the emergency brake.

"I think we need to backtrack to the night I said the 'L' word."

Claire turned to him, her arm looped over the steering wheel. She had to tell him. She had to come clean. "You don't love me." There. She'd said it. It hurt. It hurt like hell, but she'd said it.

He tried to argue, but she continued, her voice effectively drowning him out. "Oh, you *think* you love me, but you don't. Because what you feel for me isn't real. You want to know how I know that? I'll show you." She grabbed her purse, opened it up, and pulled out the voodoo doll, holding it high enough for the motel's yard light to illuminate the Doughboy's placid face.

"What the hell's that?"

"A voodoo doll. A voodoo doll of you, to be specific. And if you'll look closely, you'll see the three places where pins used to be. Here—" She pointed to the head. "And here—" She pointed to the chest. "And . . . well, here." She pointed to the crotch.

His wasn't the reaction she'd been expecting. Instead of getting mad at the way she'd tricked him and manipulated him and made him into a sex object to perform at her beck and call—whatever beck and call was—he laughed.

He *laughed.*

The idiot.

The wonderful, wonderful idiot.

"Don't you understand?" she asked, exasperated. Would she have to spell it out? "Haven't you ever seen a voodoo doll?"

"Oh, I've seen a lot of voodoo dolls."

"You have?"

"Claire, I used to live in New Orleans. Voodoo was one of the biggest cash crops."

"Then you should understand what I did. And how dishonest it was."

"I lived in New Orleans long enough to know that there was the tourist voodoo, and the real voodoo."

She poked at the top of the doll's head. "This is your hair."

"Did you burn candles while chanting a love incantation? Did you use any herbs like willow and yarrow? Did you perform the ceremony of beckoning?"

"I don't know what you're talking about."

"Exactly."

"But I'm sure I would have tried it if I'd known about it." When she went truthful, she went all the way.

He took the doll from her. "This isn't anything. It's a toy. A stuffed doll." He rolled down the window.

She screamed, jumped across the gearshift and grabbed his arm. "Don't!" She had visions of it lying in the parking lot, cars running over it.

"Claire. It won't hurt me if I throw this out."

"But what if it does?" she whispered, leaning into him, hanging on to his arm with both hands. "I don't want to risk it. Please don't. Please?"

He tossed the doll on the dashboard, rolled up the window, then wrapped both of his arms around her, pulling her close, the bulk of her winter jacket between them. He lifted her face to his and found her lips.

She sighed and relaxed into him, returning kiss for kiss.

"You smell like a motel room," she said groggily, finally able to get him back for the mothball thing.

He just laughed and kissed her some more.

"There's your proof," he said a couple of minutes later when the windows were steamed up and Claire was sweating under her heavy winter clothes.

"Hmm?"

"I still want you as much as ever. Does it ever get warm enough around here to wear fewer clothes? Wouldn't it be nice if you were wearing a dress right now? Kind of a flowing white shift with nothing under but those panties I like so well."

"In the summer, it gets warm enough to lie outside naked."

"You don't say?"

"I don't make a habit of that kind of behavior, but with the right company, it might be . . . very nice."

"I have to ask you something," he said, suddenly becoming serious. "Did you mean it when you said chess was sexy?"

"Is that what this is all about? You're trying to learn chess because I said I thought it was sexy?" She pressed her lips against his, intending that it be a quick kiss, getting lost in him all over again. "That is the absolutely sweetest thing I've ever heard. But Dylan, you don't have to play chess for me to think you're sexy."

"That's good." He slid his hands under her coat, cupping her to him. "That's what I needed to hear."

"I'm sorry I barged in on your game like that. I'm sorry I thought you were doing something illegal."

"That's okay. That's what I love about you. Your *zugzwang*."

"My what?"

"*Zugzwang*. It means you have the compulsion to act, even if it means you could worsen your position."

"*Zugzwang*."

Another chess term. She wanted to give herself over to the moment, but little things filtered their way into her subconscious. She had a mental flash. In her mind, she saw the tattoo on Dylan's arm. She'd always thought it was a horse, but now she realized it could also be a knight. And what about the way he was always tinkering with things, planning out new and more elaborate ways to make things work with his mathematical mind. Why hadn't she seen it before? The clues had been there all along, even back as far as the day she'd rescued him from the blizzard, when he'd looked up at her and mumbled something about a queen needing a knight.

"You weren't here tonight to get a chess lesson, were you?" she asked.

"No."

There was no hesitation in his answer. Was that a sign that he'd planned to tell her the truth?

"You were here to play."

"Yes."

She took it one question further. "Have you ever played professionally?"

"Yes."

"What about Daniel French? Where does he fit into all of this?"

"That's something I was going to tell you." He shifted uncomfortably. Claire had the feeling she already knew what he was about to say.

"I'm Daniel French. Dylan is my middle name. It's what my family always called me."

Why hadn't he told her? If he cared about her, why had he kept his identity a secret? "Why did you let me believe you were a criminal?"

"At first I knew that if I tried to tell you differently, you wouldn't believe me. And then, later, I guess I wanted to see if you would like me, just me, for myself and who I was, not who I was supposed to be."

She had another thought. "So who is that in there with Libby?" She was afraid she knew the answer to this one, too.

"Trevor Davis."

"The criminal. You guys traded places. I can see the advantage for Trevor, but why would you want to switch places with a criminal?"

"That . . . Well, that was more Davis's idea than mine."

That was all he said about it, about a man who'd left him for dead and taken his identity. Apparently revenge wasn't something that burned in Dylan's soul the way it did in most humans. But then, Claire had always known he wasn't like everybody else.

In the motel room, they found Trevor Davis and Libby hunched over the card table, the chess set between them, with Trevor going over the basics.

"And this horse, I mean the knight, can move over the top of things? If this square here"—she pointed—"is empty, he can do this?" She moved the piece to a new square.

"That's right," Trevor said, seeming quite pleased with his new and intrigued pupil.

"This is so interesting," Libby said, looking up from the board. "I never knew chess could be so interesting."

"Yeah." Trevor checked the bedside clock. "I've got to be back to the airport soon."

Libby slid off the bed. "Do you have to leave right away? I'm got plenty of room at my place."

Trevor looked as if he couldn't have heard her right. The poor guy obviously wasn't used to women coming on to him. Especially a woman as attractive and forward as Libby.

"Are you kidding?" he asked.

"You could teach me more fascinating chess moves."

The man actually blushed. Claire stood watching the interplay. Trevor didn't seem at all Libby's type, but you never could tell, and Libby actually seemed taken with him.

Maybe Libby had come on too strong, or maybe Trevor really did have to be somewhere like he said. Whatever the reason, he ended up packing up his chess pieces, calling a cab, and heading off into the sunrise, leaving a dejected Libby waving good-bye.

Twenty-nine

Libby had left her car at Claire's, so they all piled into the Jeep, with Claire behind the wheel, Dylan in the passenger seat, and Libby in the back with Dylan's plastic bag.

"I'd say that certainly went well," Libby said, congratulating herself, leaning forward, arms draped over the seat so her face was almost between Claire and Dylan. She kept chattering about how cute Trevor was, and how it was too bad he'd had to leave. When they got to Claire's, with an ecstatic Hallie barking and circling Dylan, Libby fished out her keys and hopped into her car, waving and blowing kisses as she drove off, finally leaving Claire and Dylan to themselves.

Two days later, Libby was pounding on Claire's door again. Before Dylan or Claire could answer, she barged in, tossing her purse down on the couch and pulling off her jacket. "I knew he should have stayed at my place. Have you two seen the news?"

They both shook their heads. Claire blushed and Dylan smiled at her. They hadn't had much time for any extracurricular activity.

Libby turned on the TV. "You have to see this."

They had to wait through some bad commercials, then the regularly scheduled programming was interrupted.

"Here we are once again with the top story of the day, or perhaps the season," said the news anchor. "The person thought to be enigmatic chess master Daniel French is actually con man and wanted criminal Trevor Davis."

"Jesus," Dylan mumbled, dropping to the couch, hands between his knees, eyes on the screen. "I should never have made him come here."

"And that's just the beginning of this bizarre, tragic tale."

"A tale. Why is it always a tale?" Claire wondered out loud.

"Shhh." Libby waved her hand.

The camera cut to a prepared, taped story. Suddenly on the screen was a shot taken from the air. A shot of mountains and snow. An airplane crash. Dylan felt sick to his stomach.

"In January, a private plane crashed in the snow-covered mountains of northern Idaho. The pilot died upon impact. One man walked away. The other is presumed dead."

The camera cut back to the studio, to the man behind the desk. "The survivor who walked away that day claimed to be reclusive chess champion Daniel French, but we've only just discovered that he is not French at all. He's none other than convicted felon Trevor Davis. Davis is an escaped prisoner wanted for fraud and embezzlement. He has confessed to leaving the severely injured French on the plane by himself, claiming to have gone for help, while at the same time stealing a dying man's identity."

They cut to an interview with the captain of the rescue team. "Is there any way the real Daniel French could have made it out of the mountains?"

The man shook his head. "He had several things against him. His injuries, of course. But he also had the depth of the snow that was already on the ground, the storm that blew in the following day, the frigid temperatures, and lack of experience."

"You didn't mention a bunch of assholes firing guns," Dylan said.

"I don't know if one of my men, experienced as they are, could have made it off the mountain under those conditions, let alone your average person."

They cut back to the news desk. "There you have it. Sad news for the world of chess."

"Is anyone still looking for Daniel French?" asked the co-anchor.

"The search was called off weeks ago," the newscaster said with just the right amount of somberness. "At this point he is presumed dead."

Libby shut off the TV. "I can't believe it. I finally find a guy I like, and he's a felon."

"Libby, you were only around him for a half hour," Claire pointed out.

"Sometimes that's all it takes." Libby grabbed her coat. "I gotta go." She stormed out like it was their fault.

And maybe it was, Dylan thought after she left.

Claire tried to get his mind off Trevor, but nothing worked. She suggested renting a movie.

Nothing he wanted to see.

Or going for a drive to the high mountains.

Not today.

Or making love.

He'd been all set to say no before she even asked the question. He had to shift gears halfway through his answer.

"No—okay."

An hour later, he was back on Trevor again. "It's my fault."

"Let me remind you that if you'd been thrown into prison instead, he'd be celebrating."

"No, he would have come forward." He rubbed his forehead. "I can't quit thinking about him getting raped by a bunch of murderers.

There has to be some way to get him into a minimum-security prison, one for white-collar criminals. I'm going to talk to a lawyer."

Before Dylan could get things lined up, Trevor ended up taking care of the problem himself.

Hardly more than twenty-four hours after his arrest, Trevor escaped from the jail where he was being held temporarily.

A couple of days after Trevor's escape, Dylan was acting moody again. Claire didn't know what to expect, but when he pulled her into his arms and asked her to go to New Orleans with him, she couldn't have been any more surprised.

"I have some things I want to pick up," he explained. "Some things I left there a long time ago."

They caught a flight out of Boise, leaving Claire's Jeep in long-term parking, and Hallie in the care of Libby. At first Claire protested about the cost of her coming along, but then Dylan explained that he could afford it. "I want you with me."

They had a layover at the Denver International Airport. It was the first really big public place he'd gone in years. Getting off the plane, walking down the narrow ramp, brought back memories of cameras flashing and reporters jamming microphones in his face.

Stepping out of the accordion ramp, he braced himself, half expecting to be bombarded by press.

Nothing happened.

Nobody recognized him.

They were passing a newspaper stand when Claire stopped him, a hand to his arm. "Is that you?" she whispered.

He followed her gaze to a rack of papers. Staring back at him was his old face, his old young face. His old innocent face. Clean-shaven, thin, dark eyes staring straight at the world.

He picked up the paper. "Yeah, that's me."

Claire leaned her cheek against his shoulder. She put out her hand, tracing a finger along the face in the paper. "You were so sweet." There was an ache in her voice. "So *young*. My God, Dylan. You were just a kid."

Dylan continued to stare at the paper, trying to see a little bit of the man he had become in the child he used to be. But it was like looking at someone else's face, a stranger's.

Peripherally, he was aware of Claire, digging into her pocket and paying for the paper.

"I was too young. It was too much too soon," he said, walking away, head bent toward a tribute that told about how the chess world was grieving over the loss of one of its greatest stars.

He'd been the same as a child star, except he hadn't had the support of parents or relatives, or even close friends.

"The whole thing overwhelmed me. I didn't know how to handle it, didn't know how to stand up for myself the way I should have. And because of that, I overreacted. All I knew how to do was run." They stopped near a flight board.

"Our plane is leaving on time." Claire looked up at him, a little smile on her face. "What?"

He was thinking how nice it was to have her there, with him. The hollow noise of people was almost deafening. The loudspeaker was announcing flight arrivals and departures. A couple of little kids were fighting over a stuffed animal. A baby was crying, and the father was jamming a pacifier into its mouth, trying desperately to calm it down.

"I like this you and me stuff," he said.

Dylan took her to the roughest part of New Orleans where whores hung out on street corners and crack heads talked to walls and peed on the sidewalk right in front of everybody.

"What are we doing?" Claire asked, sidestepping something that looked like it might be vomit.

"I used to live here."

"*Here?* As in right here?"

"A few blocks away. I used to hang out here in my free time."

"That was a long time ago, though. It's probably changed a lot, right?" She wanted him to say yes, she couldn't stand thinking of him growing up in a place like this.

"It's changed a little."

She let out a relieved sigh.

"It's maybe a little cleaner, and there aren't people shooting up in the streets."

Claire looked around, unable to imagine anyone being there by choice.

An hour later, neither of them had any cash left. They'd given it all away. "Most of them will use it to buy crack," Dylan said. "But a few might buy something to eat."

He stopped in front of a bar. He checked out the name above the door, then looked back at Claire. "Do you want to go back to the hotel?"

She shook her head and followed him inside. The place was dark, the floor sticky. Behind the bar was one of the biggest, blackest men Claire had ever seen.

"What'll it be?" he asked, hands braced on the wooden bar top.

"Hello, Jackson."

The man looked at him closer, his brow furrowed. "Do I know you?"

"It's me. French."

For a big man, he moved fast. He came around the counter, got Dylan in a huge bear hug and lifted him off the ground. "I thought you were dead, man!"

"Only to the rest of the world."

"Oh, man. It's so good to see you! Hey, I've

still got your box. I'll get it. You wait right here."

Jackson went up a short flight of stairs, then returned carrying a gray cardboard box. He put it down on the counter, and kept smiling at Dylan, shaking his head.

"You're a good guy," Dylan said. "You always had food for me. I remember how you always wanted to do more for the street people."

"Now I can. I opened two soup kitchens and built another shelter."

Dylan's eyebrows lifted. He looked around the dingy bar.

"I didn't do it on profit from this place," Jackson said, laughing. "Every year I get a check from an anonymous benefactor."

"That's great, man."

They said their good-byes. Dylan picked up the soft-edged box from the counter, looked at Claire, whose eyes were glistening just like big Jackson's, and smiled. She smiled back. Together they walked out of the bar into the bright sunlight.

At the hotel, Dylan put down the box on the bed and both he and Claire stared at it.

"So, this is what we came to New Orleans for, I take it?"

"That's right."

"Are you going to open it?" She got the distinct idea that he was afraid to.

"I don't know if I can."

She sat down behind him on the bed, her hands on his arms, her chin resting on his shoulder. "What's in it, Dylan?"

"My past." He took a deep breath.

He lifted the lid.

Earthly treasures.

The scent of things old drifted to her. There on top was a dried, crumbled rose.

"From Olivia's funeral," he said, lifting it out, crumbled pieces falling on the bed. There were photographs, faded and dusty and stained. Now that she'd seen the picture of Dylan in the paper, she could recognize him with his family, his mother, his father, his sister. Also in the box were two embroidered handkerchiefs. He lifted them to his face, inhaling. "My mother always smelled like this. I guess it's perfume."

The next thing was a chessboard—with the most beautiful, intricately carved pieces Claire had ever seen.

He passed the black knight to Claire. "This is amazing," she said, her voice a whisper. And then she realized it was Dylan's tattoo. A knight. A dark horse.

"A friend of mine made them."

She didn't have to ask. From the way Dylan was acting, and from the other contents of the box, she knew that friend was dead. He'd had so much sorrow in his life, so much sadness. She wished she could take it all away, but then if she could, he wouldn't be who he was, he wouldn't be Dylan.

She would have been bitter. He should have hated Trevor Davis. Instead, he'd agonized over his imprisonment. He should have hated New Orleans, a place that hadn't been good to him. Instead, he actually seemed glad to be there. He should have hated the world. Instead, he was facing it once more with an almost childlike wonder.

"He didn't believe in creating anything that would last more than a few days, and yet he made these. I never did get it."

"He must have done them for you. So you would have some tangible memory of who he was."

"Maybe."

"We live on in the people who have gone before us, the people who have touched our lives."

"Don't bullshit me. I'm not going to fall apart, if that's what you think."

"Dylan, it's true. Weren't your parents missionaries?"

"Yeah."

"And aren't you the anonymous benefactor?"

He didn't admit it, not in words, but his expression said, How'd you figure that out?

"I know *you*."

She knew him and understood him more

every day, loved him more every day. She knew the box wasn't the only reason he'd needed to come to New Orleans. He'd needed to see what Jackson had done with his gift. He may have spent too much time hiding in the desert, but it hadn't been idle time. He'd still managed to make a difference.

"Why are you looking at me like that?" he asked, curious, half smiling, half knowing.

"Because I love you."

Thirty

Things fell into a pattern. Claire sketched and painted during the day, and Dylan . . . well, Dylan piddled around. There was only so much wood that needed to be cut, and only so many ways to haul it in. There were only so many leaky faucets to repair, so many roofs that needed to be fixed. Even though it wasn't obvious, Claire sensed his restlessness. He was going through a transition. She just hoped she wasn't part of that transition.

One evening she found him sitting on the couch in the dark, the fire in the stove forgotten, the room cold. On his lap was the chess set Uriah had made.

She sat down beside him. "You have to go back. Chess is your life."

It might mean losing him, it might mean breaking her heart, but she loved him too much to go along with what he was doing to himself.

"I'm not ready."

"Will you ever be ready?"

"I don't know."

"You can't turn away from something that's so much a part of you."

"I was thinking that maybe I'd put an ad in the paper, start teaching chess."

That was a beginning.

The first person to show up was a ten-year-old boy named Josh who had absolutely no interest in learning to play chess. During the third lesson, when he still hadn't grasped the basic movement of the pieces, Josh finally admitted that his father had suggested the lessons, and he'd gone along with it to make his dad happy.

"Don't tell him, okay?" he begged.

"You can't keep coming here, wasting my time and your father's money," Dylan told him.

"Maybe we could do something else. Do you have any cool video games? I have this one where the players' heads get chopped off and blood goes everywhere."

Dylan looked down at the chessboard. It wasn't the one Uriah had made. This was a set Dylan had picked up at the grocery store. He looked at the knight, the queen, and the king. Sure, they were plastic, but how could Josh not feel the same sense of excitement and wonder Dylan felt when he looked at the pieces? "Do you know how old this game is?" he asked.

Josh shook his head.

Dylan figured he'd give him the benefit of the doubt. "Nobody knows for sure, but it started before the sixth century. Do you know how old that video game is you're talking about?"

"It came out this year. It's new. It's, like, really new. And I've heard they're working on another one that's supposed to be even better."

"Why play a game that's been played in feudal Europe? Why play a game that's been played during the Crusades, and by Greek philosophers, when you could be sitting in front of the television, joystick in your hand, playing something that just came out yesterday and by tomorrow will be heading for the landfill?"

Josh totally missed the sarcasm, which was probably all for the best, Dylan figured.

"Yeah. That's what I thought. Except for the landfill part." The kid was looking at him in that slightly confused way most adults had looked at Dylan all his life. How could he expect a kid to understand? If he ever had kids of his own, would they stare at him in that same way, or would they speak his language? He hoped to hell they'd speak his language, at least part of the time.

His second student was an eighty-year-old man who had always wanted to learn how to play chess. But ten minutes into the lesson, he asked, "Do you have any checkers? I like checkers. How 'bout you?"

Dylan couldn't win. On one hand, the world was moving too fast for a game that was centuries old, on the other, it was moving too slowly.

"I'm stuck between two worlds," he told Claire that night when they were lying in bed, tangled and sweet from making love, the voodoo doll that Claire refused to part with perched on the dresser, handcuffs dangling from the top railing of the bed.

Claire dropped a soft kiss on his mouth, so sweet, so tender, causing an ache in his chest. "I'm sorry."

"It's not your fault."

"That reminds me. Libby stopped by and said that she's sending over some guy who's working for her. He supposedly wants lessons."

"I can't take it anymore. These clowns are an insult to the game."

"It's too late to do anything about it. He's coming at ten o'clock."

Dylan groaned and let his head drop back on the pillow.

At exactly ten o'clock Dylan answered a knock at the door. Standing there was a kind of scrawny guy with bleached-blond hair, dark eyebrows, and one of those short beards that just covered the chin.

"Don't you recognize me?" the man asked.

"Should I?"

He stepped inside and shrugged off his jacket. "It's me. Trevor."

"You son of a bitch! You damn chameleon!" Dylan grabbed him and half lifted him off the ground. Then he shouted over his shoulder. "Claire! Claire, come down here. You aren't going to believe this!"

Claire came running and everybody started talking at once. The excitement wound down, and Trevor was finally able to explain how he'd turned himself in. "The police made it look like they'd figured it out themselves," he said, laughing. "But I just walked up and gave them my spiel and they arrested me and threw me in jail."

"*Why?*" Claire asked. "Why did you do it?"

Trevor looked from Claire to Dylan. "So he could go back. And so I could start at the bottom and work my way up. That's why I'm here. I came for lessons."

"You're working for Libby?" Claire asked as they set up the chess pieces.

Trevor actually blushed. "Yeah. She's building this wall around her place. . . ."

Dylan laughed.

He looked happier than Claire had seen him look in weeks. She backed away. And when she left the room, no one noticed.

Be careful what you wish for.

★   ★   ★

Trevor came almost every day for two months.

It was a bittersweet time, a time when everything felt so right and so good, a time Claire knew would pass.

The day came when Trevor announced that he was leaving, that he was going to take what he'd learned from Dylan and see if he could make it.

"I have a new identity. From now on I will be known as Elliot Lafayette."

"Lafayette?" Dylan asked, laughing, but Claire could see the restlessness already seeping into his eyes. "Couldn't you have picked something a little less flamboyant?"

"I want to make a splash."

Claire had a party, just the four of them. And while they joked and laughed, there was an undertone of sadness.

"I'm going to miss that little geek," Libby confessed to Claire as they stood in the kitchen sipping wine and chewing on crackers neither one of them tasted. Trevor and Dylan sat at the table in the corner, playing one last game of insanity chess.

"You'll see him again," Claire said with conviction. And she would. There was no doubt in her mind that Trevor would come back to Libby. So why didn't she feel that way about Dylan?

"Dylan is leaving, too."

"When? Why didn't he mention it?"

"He doesn't know it yet."

"Claire. Don't go stewing about something that probably won't happen."

"He has to leave."

"Don't tell him that."

"I love him. I want him to be happy."

"How about simply content. Isn't that enough?"

"Remember how I tried to give up art? How I tried to convince myself it was the right thing?"

"You were miserable."

"I didn't think it was apparent."

"You went out of your way to act like you were having a good time. That's how I knew you were miserable."

"I don't want to be this woman, waiting for her man to come back. I hate that kind of thing. It's so pathetic."

"Claire, how much wine have you had?"

Claire looked at her empty glass. She tried to remember how many times she'd refilled it, but couldn't. Libby lifted the glass from her friend's limp fingers. "That's what I thought."

There was a shout from the corner table. "You let me win, you son of a bitch."

Dylan shook his head. "I didn't. I swear."

"You let me win," Trevor said, packing up the pieces. "That's okay. Now I can go out into the world and say I beat Daniel French."

He gave Dylan a hug and a slap on the back. "Don't hide yourself forever. Life isn't about hiding. Or about running. It's about playing the game. You always have to play the game or there's no sense in being here."

They left in a flurry of confusing good-byes.

And then everything was silent.

Dylan continued to stand outside, hands shoved deep into the front pockets of his jeans, staring into the darkness in the direction Libby's car had gone. He sensed Claire beside him.

"He beat me," he finally said, stunned.

"Why are you surprised? You taught him everything you know."

"Not everything. He made a play tonight that I've never seen. It was brilliant."

"And didn't you teach him that, too? To think for himself?"

Dylan was quiet. He had to tell her, but he didn't know how.

"It's time, isn't it?"

"How did you know?"

"I know you."

"Come with me."

She shook her head. "I have my art to finish. And I don't want to be one of those women who follows her man around and in the process forgets who she is. I don't want to disappear like that."

"I wouldn't want that to happen. I want you to always be Claire."

That night they made love for what Claire feared could be the last time.

"I'll be back, Claire."

"Don't make promises you might not be able to keep. You might get out there and decide that this time the world is a pretty good fit."

"*We're* a good fit."

The night after Dylan left, Claire opened a bottle of dandelion wine, popped in her Leonard Cohen tape, then sat on the floor, her back against the couch. A minute later, Hallie came walking over, her head low. Heaving a dog sigh, she plopped down on the floor next to Claire, resting her head on Claire's leg.

Thirty-one

At first, Dylan wrote. In his letters, he told Claire how much he missed her. He told her how, after his initial return to the chess world, interest in him quickly waned. A seventeen-year-old grand master was news, a thirty-year-old grand master was old news.

What he didn't say, but Claire knew as truth, was that he no longer needed a retreat, because the world was no longer nipping at his heels.

Claire completed her sketches and watercolors for the card line. She mailed them in. Three weeks later, she called her agent from the same phone she'd used the day she found out Cardcity wanted to sign her.

"They love everything," John said.

"That's great."

"You don't sound as excited as I thought you would."

"I have kind of a headache." A heartache, actually.

"Well, call me later and we'll talk more. And Claire—get a phone."

"Yeah, I will."

"No you won't."

"You're right."

She hung up. Would she ever feel better? Would this huge empty feeling in her stomach, in her chest, ever go away?

Spring turned into summer.

Since Claire only rented the cabin for the cheaper, winter rate, she packed her things, preparing to move. She hadn't heard from Dylan in a month. Trevor—a.k.a. Elliot Lafayette—called Libby almost every night. He sent her flowers and sappy poems. Trevor was doing a lot of winning. But Dylan was in a class by himself. Nobody could touch him.

When Claire's editor from Cardcity heard that Claire was moving, she tried to talk her into coming to New York, where she could work more closely with the card company. Her agent thought it was a good idea too.

Instead, Claire ended up renting an upstairs apartment in downtown Fallon. In three months, when the tourist season was over, she would move back to the cabin. She had to be close to nature. How could she be a nature artist in New York City?

*   *   *

Dylan pulled up in front of Claire's, jumped out of the rental car, and hurried to fling open the cabin door.

Standing inside were two people, a man and a woman, he'd never seen before. Understandably, they both looked quite alarmed.

"Where's Claire?"

"There's no Claire here. You must have the wrong cabin."

"*You* have the wrong cabin. This is Claire's cabin."

The man and woman looked at each other, then at him. "Maybe you're looking for the person who rents this place in the off-season."

Before Dylan had left, he'd tried to talk Claire into getting a phone.

"You know where to find me," she'd said.

Why hadn't Claire told him she would be moving in the summer? He hadn't even thought about the possibility of her not being there when he returned. "Do you know where she went? Where she moved to?"

They shook their heads. "We're from Omaha. We come here every summer. But the place is always empty when we arrive."

"I'm sorry." He backed away. "Sorry."

He'd only been to Libby's once so he had a little trouble finding the place, plus he was in panic mode. Was everything okay with Claire's Cardcity contract? Had she gotten her drawings done? Turned in on time? Had they liked them?

Disliked them? Canceled her contract? Or maybe they'd loved them so much that she'd moved to New York.

Shit.

Why hadn't he come back earlier?

Time had gotten away from him. One game had led to another and another. It had felt so good, so damn *right* to be doing what he was supposed to be doing that he'd lost track of time.

But Claire. In all the time he'd been away, he'd never quit thinking about her, never quit wishing he could see her, touch her, hold her.

He found the lane that led to Libby's house. On either side were KEEP OUT, PRIVATE PROPERTY signs. And if that didn't intimidate anyone, there was a huge locked iron gate at the end of the lane.

He talked to Libby through an intercom that kept cutting out. He was ready to climb the damn gate when Libby stepped out the front door, barefoot, dressed in baggy camouflage pants and a brown T-shirt.

He jammed his fingers through his damp hair. He was sweating like hell. "Where's Claire?"

"Hi to you, too."

"Yeah, hi."

Done with that, he got back to the problem, the big problem. "Where the hell's Claire?" He tried not to shout, but from the look on Libby's face, he was afraid he hadn't succeeded.

"She's living in town. Above Electric Iguana. It's a club."

He turned and lunged toward the car.

"Thank you!" Libby shouted after him.

He waved a hand in the air, but didn't take the time to look back.

A half hour later he was walking up a narrow flight of stairs to knock on a door painted with heavy green enamel.

From inside came the sound of excited barking, then frantic scratching on the door.

Hallie.

He tried to talk to her through the locked door, but that just got her more stirred up. He left, hoping she would calm down after he was gone.

Downstairs he found a guy cleaning the bar. In one corner a band was setting up their instruments. "Cool tattoo," one of the band members said, inching past him.

Dylan glanced at his arm. "Thanks," was his distracted answer. "Have you seen Claire?" he asked the guy behind the bar.

"What day is this?"

"Thursday. It's Thursday."

"I think she teaches painting classes on Thursdays."

"Painting classes."

"Yeah."

All along, Dylan had imagined Claire waiting for him, looking just the way he'd left her, just where he'd left her, doing just what she'd been doing those last days, working on her watercolors for the card company. This threw him. She wasn't supposed to move. She wasn't supposed to be living in town, above a bar called Electric Iguana, and she wasn't supposed to be teaching.

"The classes are out by Fallon Lake. Everybody takes their own easel and sits out there and paints the water and the mountains and crap."

Dylan drove halfway around the lake before he found a bunch of brightly dressed people in big hats sitting in front of easels. It wasn't until he got closer that he realized one of the artists was licking the paint off her brush.

And when he stepped from the car, he saw that the students had quite a bit of age on them. That's when it dawned on him that they were nursing-home residents.

Even though the temperature must have been at least eighty degrees, one of the residents wore a goofy crocheted hat just like the one Claire had.

He walked closer and saw that it wasn't a nursing-home resident, but Claire, trying to maintain control of her students but losing ground fast.

"Please, Mrs. Dottingham. Paint the paper, not the easel. And Henrietta, don't eat the paint. When we're done here, we'll get ice cream."

"At the drugstore soda fountain?"

"We'll go to Dairy Delight."

"I like the soda fountain."

"It's not there any—" She stopped in midsentence, her gaze freezing on Dylan.

She looked good in summer clothes, he decided. He was even getting used to the goofy hat.

"Dylan."

She was wearing beige shorts and a white sleeveless top. On her feet were hiking boots. She was tan and healthy-looking. It didn't look as if she'd been pining away for him.

"I went by your cabin and found out you don't live there anymore. Why didn't you tell me you'd moved?"

"I didn't have any way to get in touch with you." Plus, I wasn't sure you'd care, seemed to be her unspoken words.

This wasn't going at all the way he'd imagined. He'd expected her to throw herself into his arms. He'd expected her to kiss him, be glad to see him. Instead, she wasn't even looking at him. Instead, her head was bent and she was fiddling with the paintbrush in her hand, seeming to find it more fascinating than his return.

He took a step back, not knowing what to say. Maybe she'd met somebody else. Or maybe she'd just lost interest in him. He didn't know how to react. The future without Claire . . . it wouldn't be a future at all.

"Maybe I'll see you later," he said, stupefied. He'd lost everybody he ever cared about. Why not Claire, too?

Hurt.

God, he hurt like hell. Claire. Claire, *I love you.*

She finally looked up. "You're leaving? But you just got here."

"You're busy. I'll catch you later."

"When? Where?"

"I don't know."

All he knew was that he had to get in his car and drive. Away from there, away from the pain. "At your apartment," he lied, knowing he couldn't go back there, knowing this was it. It was over. He started to walk away, when she called after him. He slowed and turned around.

"I don't want to hold you down," she said, catching up with him. "I'm so afraid I'll hold you down."

"What are you talking about?"

"You've just gotten your life together. I don't want to mess you up."

Was that what this was all about? "What I have out there—none of it means anything without you. You. *You* are my life." He didn't get it. How could she have thought any differently? "I told you I was coming back."

"You were gone so long."

He should have come back sooner. He should have written more. He was so certain of their love that he hadn't questioned their time apart and what it might mean to Claire. "Three months. I was gone three months."

"I know."

He'd spent almost a decade in the desert. To him, three months wasn't even something that could be measured, it was that small. But for Claire . . . He could see that for someone who lived in the moment, three months might as well have been a lifetime.

"Men have walked out of my life before," she explained. "I used to tell myself, He'll be back. But then I learned to tell myself, He won't be back so quit moping around. Get on with your life. Before, I was able to do that. And as time passed, my memory became fuzzy and I realized that I was better off by myself."

This didn't sound good.

"But it was different with you. The ache never went away. It just kept getting worse."

"That's what I like to hear."

"That I've been in pain?"

"That you missed me. It's so weird. It's like you're everybody and everything I've known and loved . . . yet at the same time, there are so many things about you that are uniquely you. Your sense of humor. The way you just dive into life. Where some people would stand around, analyzing things from every angle, checking out the pros and cons while the years dwindle away, you jump. You have this wonderful ability to live in the moment. And when I'm around you, I can be a part of that. I can live in the moment, too."

She shook her head, her eyes glistening. "I'm not that person," she confessed. "I wish I were, but I'm not."

"You are. You live life the way I can only

imagine, the way I can only do through chess. With reckless abandon. With unrequited joy."

He could tell she was thinking, looking back.

"Don't you see?" she said, "I'm that person when you're around. When I'm with you, I'm stronger. There is more life in me. It's not me. It's you."

He understood what she was saying, because he felt the very same thing. He was more when he was around her. He was more alive. He was smarter. Funnier. *More.*

"Together," he said, smiling, "We're one damn bright star." He pulled her into his arms and kissed her right there in front of her entire art class.

Nobody even noticed.

"I know this isn't really the place to ask—" He glanced around at her students, then back at her. "Well, maybe it's the perfect place. Will you grow old with me?"

Thirty-two

"I feel just silly as hell holding this flower."

Dylan was lying in a meadow, bees buzzing around him, a wildflower in his hand, while Claire sat a few feet away, sketchpad on her bent knees, drawing pencil in hand. To her left was a picnic basket with the remnants of their half-eaten lunch and what was left of Grandma Maxfield's bottle of plain white grape juice.

It had been two weeks since Dylan's return, and in that time they'd discussed many things, one of them the possibility of buying the rental cabin. Whatever happened, they knew they wanted to stay in Fallon. Their work would take them both away at times, but Fallon would be a place they could come back to, a place untouched by four lanes and discount chains. It was a place where people stared at you because you were a stranger, not because you'd had lunch at the White House. Dylan had sought anonymity half his life; in Fallon anonymity had found him.

"I should have had you take off your shirt," Claire said, exaggerated regret in her voice as she moved the pencil lightly across the paper.

"There's no way I'd pose with my shirt off, holding a damn flower."

Claire's confidence was growing. She still had moments of self-doubt, times when her heart would fill with panic and she wondered if she could draw another picture, if she had any talent at all. When that happened, Dylan would hold her and kiss her and tell her that self-doubt wasn't all that bad, that it made a person try harder. And he would point out that it was better than thinking she was the greatest thing that ever happened to the art world. Self-doubt kept a person humble, and he was a firm believer in humility.

"Are you almost done?" he asked again. "I can't hold this pose any longer."

She made a final sweep across the paper. She would detail it later, back at the apartment. "That's good enough."

He let out a tired sigh and fell back on the ground, his hand to his stomach, one leg bent, one straight.

"Don't you want to see it?"

"I don't know why you insisted on drawing a picture of me. I didn't think you drew people."

"I don't."

He took the tablet from her hand. He stared at it for a long time, then tossed it gently aside.

On the tablet was a drawing of a solitary bee, nothing more.

"You brat."

She laughed. She was still laughing when he attacked her, throwing himself on her, rolling her to the ground. "I have shit big love for you," he said.

"You are so romantic."

His mouth found hers. His kiss was deep and sweet and tender.

"It's finally gotten warm enough for less clothing," he said in between kisses.

"I thought you didn't want to take off your shirt," she reminded him.

"I changed my mind."

"And now you want me to draw you nude? That's an idea. I've been looking for a subject so I could use this new shade called In the Buff."

"I don't think that's what Cardcity meant in your contract where it says 'drawings of the natural kind.'"

"It doesn't say that."

"Sure it does. Right after it says that when you draw, you have to leave your underwear at home."

"How do you know I'm wearing any now?"

"I'll let you know in just a minute."

He smiled at her in that sexy way of his, then kissed her and said, "In chess, there's something called pure mate."

"Chess is so much multidimensional thinking. I'll never fully grasp it. I can only focus on one thing at a time, on what's happening at the moment."

"That's what I love about you," Dylan said. "I'll never be able to draw like you, but that's okay. It's just that sometimes things are easier for me to explain in chess terms."

"Are you trying to tell me something?" she asked, smiling.

"Pure mate is when every piece makes sense, when every piece has a reason for being where it is. It's something that doesn't happen very often, and when it does, it's profound."

There in the middle of the lush meadow, an ultra-blue sky as his backdrop, Dylan broke her heart and put it back together again, all in a space of two seconds. How could love, real love, hurt so much?

"That's what you are to me," he said. "My pure mate."